DURING MOTHER'S ABSENCE

DURING MOTHER'S ABSENCE

MICHÈLE ROBERTS

Published by VIRAGO PRESS Limited 1993
20–23 Mandela Street, Camden Town, London NW1 OHQ

*A CIP catalogue record for this book is available from the
British Library*

Printed and bound in Great Britain by
Mackays of Chatham PLC, Chatham, Kent

Acknowledgements:

'*Une Glossaire*/A Glossary' first appeared in *More Tales* (Journeyman
Press 1988); 'Anger' in *The Seven Deadly Sins* (Serpent's Tail 1988);
'Charity' in *The Seven Cardinal Virtues* (Serpent's Tail 1990); 'Fish' in
Colours of a New Day (Lawrence & Wishart 1990); 'Your Shoes' in *Give
Me Shelter* (Bodley Head 1991); 'The Bishop's Lunch' was first broadcast
on Radio Four and published in *Telling Stories* (BBC Publications,
1991); 'Taking it Easy' was also first broadcast on Radio Four and
published in *Woman's Journal* (1991); 'God's House' first appeared in *God*
(Serpent's Tail 1992).

Author's Note:

Most of these stories would not have been written if they hadn't been commissioned. My grateful thanks, therefore, to Alison Fell, Stephen Hayward, Sarah Lefanu, Duncan Minshull. I should also like to thank Caroline Dawnay, Lennie Goodings and Jim Latter, for their help and encouragement. Thanks too to the *Tales* group, Zoë Fairbairns, Sara Maitland, Valerie Miner and Michelene Wandor, whose existence meant that '*Une Glossaire*/A Glossary' got written.

For Sam and Leo

Contents

ANGER

Once upon a time, there was a red-haired country-woman called Bertrande living with her husband, Guillaume Tarentin, in their small house tucked into the side of a steep hill in Provence. Further down the pebbly track which led as far as their stone porch and nowhere else was a small orchard of apple and apricot trees, and, beyond that, quite a way down, two or three other small houses in which their neighbours lived. Right at the bottom of the hill was the village itself. Guillaume always said he liked living so high up, on account of the peace and quiet. The neighbours said it was so Bertrande could shout at him without anybody hearing. The neighbours added that Bertrande also liked being able to look down her big nose at everyone else.

1

This was literally true. When she hung the washing out in the mornings, the neighbours, if they craned their necks, could see her look up at the vast sky over her head, gaze at the hillside sheering on up above her, and then stare down at the roofs of their own houses. She had an odd rigid posture always, and at these moments would wrap her fists in her apron. Then up on to tiptoe she would go, still staring down at them, until you would have thought her legs and feet must be made of wood.

Guillaume was well-off by village standards. He and Bertrande could afford to eat their own produce, once the landlord had taken his share, not just sell it all and subsist on bread and root vegetables as the very poorest did. They ate eggs from their own chickens, and killed and boiled the same fowls when these got too old for laying; they could afford to buy olive oil to dip their bread into; if they only ate roast meat on big feast days well at least they could afford bones for soup; and Bertrande, like all the women of the village, was skilled at stretching a little a long way. What was left over from one day got turned into something else the next. Likewise, she had the knack of making clothes and utensils out of odd materials. The ticking that covered her goose-feather quilts served also to make shirts and chemises for herself and her husband; earthenware flowerpots held her wooden spoons and spatulas and tin ladles; she cut up bits of old felt to make slippers and boots. She saved everything, and found a use for it. Bits of string, knotted together, mended chair seats and baskets; she grew flowers in old saucepans, which she then stuck in a row on the windowsill; out of old boxes she made cupboards and stools; out of old cardboard she made patches for broken windows, mats for the kitchen floor of trodden earth, trays on which to store vegetables.

Thrift and good housekeeping were all very well, the neigh-bours thought, but Bertrande went too far. She was seen at Mass with chicken feathers, not ribbons, stuck in her shawl for decoration. The holy water stoup hung from a nail in the kitchen held salt. Surely her cheeks were sometimes redder than nature intended? Why, even in summer, did she swaddle herself in long heavy clothes, and shiver? Why, when she came down to the village once a week for market, was she sometimes heard singing songs that no one else knew? Sometimes she did not come down at all, and it was Guillaume who had to take her place, with his heavy baskets of fruit and vegetables, amongst the other women. Kindly, they looked away from him, and only shrugged to one another. They knew that when Bertrande should have been about her work in house and garden she was sometimes to be seen wandering on the hillside collecting wild flowers. Not to dry them for tisanes, oh no; she pressed them, stuck them on squares of sugar paper, and hung them on the wall. They felt sorry for her husband and were not surprised when after the market packed up he would vanish into the dark little village bar and get roaring drunk before staggering back up the hill.

Bertrande's hands were the largest of any woman's in the village, broad and red, marked with chilblains in winter, seamed with dirt in spring, often puckered with scars and scorch blisters, for she was clumsy in her work much of the time, didn't seem to learn from mistakes. Her hands were capable though, when they wanted to be. When it was a question of money. Her hands could gesture well when she wanted to drive a hard bargain over the price of her fat sweet tomatoes; her hands could seize and wring a goose's neck in seconds; her hands could force open a goose's stubborn beak and stuff it with grain to fatten it well; her hands

3

could slaughter ducks and butcher lambs; her thick fingers could sort coins into shining piles of silver in a twinkling. But what you never saw Bertrande's hands doing was caressing a child. Married for ten years, she appeared incapable of conceiving an heir.

The neighbours pitied Bertrande for this calamity. They conceded the pride that would not let her discuss it, even while they deplored it. They were ready to offer suggestions and remedies, but Bertrande refused to talk about it. She hardly spoke to them at all. This was odder than ever, the neighbours thought, when you considered that Bertrande was well known, in other ways, to be a noisy woman. She suffered from bad dreams at night, they knew, for she often woke her neighbours with her yells. They could hear her nag her husband when he came home drunk; her screams carried down the hillside. She quarrelled with Guillaume frequently for no good reason; the neighbours, pruning their apple trees or digging their vegetable plots, could hear her cursing him in her guttural voice. They were used to the racket she made.

So when at last she fell pregnant, and turned even more sullen and quiet with them, the village women were not so much relieved as worried. They hadn't noticed her belly swelling for a good few months, hidden as it was under her heavy black clothes. When they did, and joked with her about it, she flinched away, grumbling. She wouldn't accept offers of help and advice from the other women, who were hurt by this. At last they could welcome her as one of themselves, yet she snubbed every attempt at friendliness. Once, the midwife, meeting her in the little cemetery next to the church, reached out and patted Bertrande's belly, and the younger woman turned on her and hissed.

Everyone knew, of course, that Bertrande had come to live

with her husband from a far-off village, right over the other side of the hill. So they were prepared to make certain allowances for a stranger, and indeed, they always had. And pregnant women were known to behave oddly, to have strange fancies, to crave strange foods. But this behaviour was too proud and angry to pass unnoticed. So the anxious village women began to watch her even more closely.

In her fifth month of pregnancy, Bertrande was spotted in the woods digging up certain roots that were well known to bring on young women's monthly flows, and indeed were prescribed by the midwife for just this reason. In her sixth month of pregnancy, Bertrande was observed helping her husband in their upper field to clear it of rocks and boulders preparatory to ploughing: she picked up the heaviest possible rocks and lugged them to the edge of the hill, where it sheered off into a steep cliff, and tipped them over one by one, grunting like a pig with the effort. That Sunday, after Mass, the priest remonstrated with Guillaume. He should not let his wife roam so far from home into the woods to collect roots that could do her harm if she ate them. He should not have decided to clear the upper field, at last, at just this time. Certainly his wife's labour was essential to his making a living, no one would dispute that, but still, there were limits that should not be passed. Guillaume listened, and sighed. Then he beckoned his wife over from where she stood grumpy and silent among the other women, and took her back up the hill. That night, for the first time since the young couple had come to live there, the neighbours heard the sound of sobbing coming from Guillaume's house.

In her seventh and eighth months, Bertrande seemed calmer. She still spoke little, but she went about her usual work with her old doggedness, and was even heard once or twice singing some of her peculiar songs. But in the lulls at market, when customers were few and there was a chance to gossip and relax, she did not occupy herself stitching clothes for the baby. What are you going to wrap it in? the other women asked her: one of those old sacks you're so fond of making cushions out of? a piece of cardboard? Bertrande threw her arms in the air and laughed loudly, and a kitchen knife fell out of her sleeve and clattered on the cobblestones under the market stall.

The baby came two weeks early, on midwinter night. The midwife, sweating up the hill through the deep snow, got to the house to find two of the neighbours sitting with the labouring woman, one on each side of her big bed, and their husbands offering Guillaume tots of potato brandy in the kitchen below. Each time his wife cried out, Guillaume drank another glass of brandy. Tears ran out of the corners of his red-rimmed eyes, and he crashed his fists on to the tabletop in time to the rhythm of the shouts from above. The midwife bathed Bertrande's face, and encouraged her. Outside, the snow fell. The men stoked the fire in the kitchen, and crouched over it, hating that room above and the pain in it. They kicked the dogs who whined to get closer to the warm red flames, and they played cards, and drank potato brandy until they fell asleep and did not have to listen any more. The newborn's thin wail interrupted their dreams of suffering, and they woke, and looked at each other blearily, then got up clumsily and knelt down on the cold mud floor and thanked God.

Guillaume went shyly upstairs to see his son. The son, however, was a daughter.

— Never mind, his two friends consoled him when he came back downstairs: better luck next time. We'll drink her health anyway.

6

The midwife, who was like most of the others a kind woman when she could afford to be, came every day to see Bertrande and the child, as did the two neighbours, who made pots of lentil soup and cleaned the house and kept the fire going while the three men dug paths through the snow to the stables and saw after the animals. The women clucked and shook their heads over Bertrande's housekeeping arrangements. Never before, they remonstrated with each other, had they known such a slut, one who kept a stack of wax crayons and a drawing-book in her larder, whose linen chest contained a litter of chestnuts and corks and dried berries threaded on strings, who had decorated the wall behind the privy with her own finger and palm prints, and who had hidden a pack of Tarot cards at the bottom of the flour bin. Still, they were so happy running their fingers through worn patches in the best towels, and examining the top of the high mantelpiece for dust, and wondering whether the inky scrawls on bits of paper stuffing the draughty gaps in the windows were spells or illicit love letters, that when they went up to the bedroom to check how the new mother was doing they were in a cheerful frame of mind and could be patient with her.

For Bertrande found it very difficult to feed her baby. Indeed, the women whispered, you could say she didn't want to. She needed a lot of encouragement to do it, and it seemed that even when she did her milk was thin and did not adequately nourish the baby, who cried a lot in a fretful sort of way that was hard to bear. Still, the baby, who at first had seemed weak and sickly, was at least surviving. In no time at all, the women counselled Bertrande, in a couple of days, say, the little one would take to the breast without such fuss, and then the milk would flow more easily and Bertrande would relax and all would be well.

7

The crying drove Guillaume from the house, you could see that. He could be of little use, of course, for the women were there with his wife doing everything, and it was not a man's place anyway. He took to neglecting even the jobs he could have been doing in that bad weather, bits of mending and glueing and general re-fixing, and the house grew even more tumbledown around him. He did the bare minimum for the animals, then slouched out, saying he was going down to the neighbours to see if they needed him for anything. The two husbands reported that they never saw him. It was clear that he slipped and slithered down the snowy path to the village bar most evenings, for he would return just as the two women were about to leave for their own homes, wet through and smelling of brandy. He was suffering, but no one could ask him why, for that was not their way. No one had words for what was going on, and they never had had. The priest might have had words for it, but he never came up the hill in the bad weather, and the women did not dare suggest that Guillaume go and visit him. They watched Bertrande turn her head away when her husband came into the bedroom and hovered by the cradle, they saw her look contemptuously at him as he slunk out, they saw her mouth set hard and her big red hands make lumpy fists under the sheet. She wouldn't say the rosary with them of an evening. She wouldn't let them touch the baby with holy water in case the devil carried its soul away before they got it down to the church for a christening. Yet it was well known that these practices were efficacious. The women sighed. With such a mother, what prospect was there for the child?

After a week, there came a thaw. The two husbands took it as a signal to call their wives home, where they were much needed, and the midwife departed to a nearby village to attend another lying-in.

Bertrande and Guillaume were left alone with each other and the baby.

When the thing happened, it took a while for the villagers to make sense of it. As the neighbours explained to the people living lower down the hill, Guillaume was in such a state of anxiety when he came sliding down the muddy track to their door that for a while they could get nothing out of him, only curses and weeping. They gave him brandy, and that steadied him. Then he told them. But even then he was so incoherent and muddled that his worried listeners had to piece his story together for themselves, and, once the news had flown down the hill and began to be passed round the village, no one could be quite sure of the right order of Guillaume's words any more, let alone what had actually happened.

Guillaume said the fire was out. No, Bertrande said that the fire was out. She was cold, and so was the baby. She needed fire. She needed to be warm. She wanted to go back to bed, not to sit in a cold kitchen with no fire. Guillaume went out to the shed to fetch wood for the fire. The fire was not out. The fire was near Bertrande. Bertrande was near the fire. She made more fire with the poker. The flames licked up. She held the baby to the fire to make it warm, like the fire inside her. She held the fire to the baby. Bertrande dropped the baby in the fire. She said it was not an accident.

Later, the priest tried to sort out the right words. Bertrande. The baby fell in the fire by accident.

But everyone knew that that was not really true. And the priest was not there so how could he know? And Bertrande was never seen in church again, so it was clear she had not made her confession: he had not found out that way.

The child lived. Miraculously, the women said, crossing themselves, her little face was unscathed when Guillaume picked her off the glowing embers and tore the smouldering wrappings off. Though she had been dropped face downwards, only the skin on the uppermost part of her body had been touched by the red ashes burning through. Though the new skin would grow again, it would be shiny and angry and red. But she would not die.

The priest came puffing up the hill to christen the child. They named her Melusine. No one knew where the name came from, and no one dared ask. Guillaume simply said that it would be so. Bertrande went to bed and stayed there and was silent. They brought the child to her to be fed, and they watched her to make sure that she did not try to harm it again. Downstairs in the kitchen, drinking unhappy toasts to the bandaged newborn, they whispered to each other that Bertrande was a monster.

After that, the midwife sent for her sister, who was unmarried, to come and keep house for Guillaume and to keep an eye on Bertrande, who remained in bed and would not get up. Nor would she speak to anyone. Luckily, the midwife's sister was a cheerful girl, who was not affected by the atmosphere in the house. She did not mind drunken men, being used to them, and when one night, on returning from the village bar, Guillaume pulled open the front of her blouse, she only giggled a bit. She told her sister all about it, and her sister told her to be careful. People would talk.

Bertrande would not talk. She heard the whisperings, the women knew, which sidled up through the floorboards, down the chimney, in at the window: they did not always bother to lower their voices. It was right she should know what they thought.

They always said the same thing. They watched the words settle inside her, souring her stomach so that she could not eat or drink. They watched the words gnaw at her soul, worrying at it, shredding it to rags and holes. They watched her feed what was left of her soul into her daughter's rosy mouth which ardently sucked it in. The baby seemed to use up her mother's strength: she flourished, while Bertrande grew weaker day by day. Or perhaps, the women whispered, the devil was claiming his own. You could see how Bertrande did not resist him; she drifted easily towards her death. Guillaume slept in the kitchen now. One morning, awakened early by the baby's cries, he stumbled upstairs to rouse his wife to feed her, and found Bertrande cold and stiff against the big square pillow. Her hair, he told the neighbours later, was unplaited and loose all round her face, and there was a thick strand of it caught between her lips.

The priest decided that since Bertrande had not been arraigned and convicted of any crime, charity dictated that she be buried in the corner of the churchyard, close enough to the church to be included in the company of the righteous, and at a sufficient distance not to cause offence. It was a poor funeral, people said afterwards: like a pauper's. They understood why Guillaume would not allow any flowers, and why he did not invite them back to his house afterwards, and why he marked the grave with a plain cross made of cheap wood with no words cut on it other than his wife's name. What else could he have done? Bunched in their best black, separated from him by six feet of respect, they watched him stand, pale and dry-eyed, at the grave's edge, while the priest read out the words of prayers that were snatched from his mouth by the wind and soon lost.

Then Guillaume needed a new wife. He needed her hands labouring in the kitchen and the fields and the garden, he needed her broad back to help him bear his sorrow and

11

shame, he needed her cunt in his bed at night. He needed her eyes never to look into his in the way that Bertrande's had. So, since his friends and the priest went on at him that he should regularise the position in which the midwife's sister found herself, he seduced her properly and then married her. Everybody agreed it was for the best. The wet-nurse jiggled Melusine up and down in her arms, and the plump red-haired baby laughed with pleasure.

Melusine must always have known, Pierre Caillou thought, the story of her mother's life and death. It must have grown her, have shaped her. But it was not this old scandal that made him notice her particularly: he grew interested in Melusine only when he first realised she had a secret.

Pierre Caillou was the village schoolmaster. He was an educated man, who had left the village to study fifty kilometres away in the great city none of his compatriots had ever seen, and who had returned full of ideas and compassion, determined to give his neighbours' children the chance to learn how to read and write and to lead better lives than those of their parents. After five years of trying to run an elementary school on proper scientific lines, he admitted defeat, acquired a stooped back, and contented himself with teaching those children whose parents let them attend school when they were not needed in the fields or in the house. He had a lot of free time, with so few scholars. So he became himself a student again, first of local folklore and superstition, and then, more precisely, of the customs, morals and beliefs of his fellow villagers. They resented him for this, and he did not blame them. He knew he was privileged, doing no physical work, and with his schoolmaster's stipend topped up by the rents from two farms he had inherited from his parents. He had no friends, though he occasionally played backgammon with the priest on those nights when loneliness drove him to accept the old curé's stupid tolerance of his atheism. He slept at the school, on a truckle bed set up in his office. At night he would extinguish the fire, bundle himself in a grey woollen blanket, and scribble in his notebook. He had a row of these on the mantelpiece, all identical, cheap flimsy notebooks bound in brown cloth.

At fourteen years old, Melusine was still coming to school each morning. It kept her out of mischief, Guillaume said to Pierre, shrugging his shoulders, it kept her from getting in the way, and if she picked up some useful knowledge, well, all to the good. She could do his accounts for him and prove her usefulness that way. Madame Tarentin agreed: these days, people needed a bit of booklearning. And Melusine already knew most of what there was to know about tending a house. She could afford to put in some time at school. She could help her parents in the afternoons, when the school was closed.

Melusine always sat in the corner of the classroom, near the black iron stove, the best place because the warmest, which she had won on account of being the oldest scholar, and a position she defended with kicks and biting when necessary. Yet she also liked it, Pierre Caillou thought, because the angle of the wall and the bulge of the stove cut her off from the other children, and because she could look out of the window beside her at the short row of pollarded limes edging the path up to the church and watch the comings and goings of people and animals and birds. She daydreamed a lot, and he often had to reprove her, for her inattention was an affront to his authority over the other children. Yet she was a good student: she could read and write well, unlike most of the others, and she was quick at sums when she put her mind to it.

One day he spied on her from behind, peering over her shoulder before she could run the sponge over her slate. He had set the children a geography test, commanding them to draw a map of their province complete with rivers and towns. But Melusine had chosen to sketch, in her coloured chalks, the portrait of some mythical creature she must have seen in a picturebook somewhere: a wild being of the woods, half-man, half-beast, covered from head to toe in thick curly fur, and with little breasts peeping out that proved her to be female.

– What's this? Pierre Caillou asked, reaching his hand over Melusine's shoulder and grabbing her slate.

He moved round in front of her in order to see her face. It was dreamy and contented; she was still in her daydream, her pleasure. He realised that she was not as ugly as he had always thought. It was when she was afraid that she grew ugliness as an extra and protective skin. Still absorbed in her drawing, still attached to it, she was soft, shining.

– Where did you copy this from? he persisted: where did you find it?

Melusine hesitated.

– Nowhere, she said: I just drew it.

He reached for the sponge. She watched him. She was impassive, hard again. He touched the sponge to the slate. Her face twitched.

– In the mirror, she blurted: I saw it in the mirror.

– Stay behind at twelve o'clock, he commanded: I want to get to the bottom of this.

It was cold in the little office where he slept. Melusine stood by the open door, shivering. Noticing, he gestured her in, shut the door behind her, and lit the fire. Normally he never permitted himself a fire in the morning. Only ever at night.

14

He sat on the truckle bed and she stood in front of him where he ordered her to stand.

– Take your clothes off, he said: show me.

Melusine frowned.

– Don't be silly, he scolded: I am your teacher, there can be nothing wrong. Do as I tell you.

She stood, stiff, between his knees. So he undressed her himself, laying her black school overall carefully on the bed beside him, undoing the buttons of her smock one by one, tugging the rough linen chemise over her head, till he had her naked to the waist.

He knew, of course, as did everyone in the village, that she had been burnt as a baby, and that the midwife had said that the skin would grow back but would be shiny and puckered and red, that she would be grotesque in the place where the women of that country were smooth milky white. What he had not expected were the little breasts. He had thought her too young. What he had not expected was the thick, silky thatch of bright red hair that curled from her neck down around her breasts and on down to her waist.

He stretched his hand out. It shook a little. He touched the red mat of hair, and then her breasts, first one and then the other. Melusine tried to step backwards and he gripped her between his knees.

– Don't be frightened, he told her: I won't hurt you.

He suddenly found that he wanted her to want his caresses. He had never touched a woman before. He wanted her to unbend towards him, as though he were the fire and she could warm herself at him.

– Melusine, he demanded: when did this happen?

She hung her head and mumbled. Even when he laid her

15

gently on the bed and lifted up her skirts, she said nothing he could understand.

– I'll take you home, he decided afterwards: I must speak to your father about this.

The Tarentins were obliged to ask him in to share their midday meal. All the time he was reaching for more bread, or accepting a second plate of cabbage soup, or wiping his greasy mouth on the back of his hand, he was watching Melusine, who sat at the far end of the table and of course said nothing. In those days children did not speak in front of their elders, and Pierre Caillou approved of this. It allowed him to speak of Melusine as though she were not there. His questions, however, alarmed Madame Tarentin, and she sent her stepdaughter outside to sweep the yard. For a moment he saw Melusine's moon face glimmer sadly at the little window; then her father shook his fist at the glass and she disappeared.

Some months before, the parents told him, Melusine was discovered scrubbing herself under the pump, trying to get rid of the unsightly growth of hair that had appeared overnight on the scarred skin of her chest. At the same time they had not only caught her rootling in the old wooden chest into which Bertrande's things had been thrown after her death, but had discovered that she had used the stubs of wax crayon she found there to produce drawings of a hideous sort. No amount of beatings administered by her worried father could stop her drawing. No amount of herbal poultices applied by her worried stepmother could get rid of the thick growth of hair. In the end they used Guillaume's cut-throat razor and shaved it off. But the hair had simply grown back the next month, and she had gone on making her drawings on every scrap of cardboard she could lay her hands on. The most disturbing aspect of

16

the whole business, the parents admitted, was that the hair regularly disappeared of its own accord after four or five days, and reappeared with equal regularity a month later. Bertrande, that unhappy woman, and here they both crossed themselves, had delivered herself of a monster.

Pierre Caillou and Melusine were married soon afterwards, just as soon as the banns had been properly read and Melusine had finished hemming the last sheet and nightgown in her trousseau which, like all the girls in the village, she had started sewing at an early age. She didn't bring Pierre Caillou much, for her parents had little money to spare that winter, and he used this fact to put pressure on them to agree to the marriage. They were relieved, he could see, to get their daughter settled with the only man in the village who could possibly have accepted her.

– Now she's got you to look after her, Madame Tarentin told him: she'll be all right at last. I shan't have to worry about what will become of her any more.

– It's right she should marry and go with you, Guillaume said: poor thing.

They made only one condition. Pierre must promise never to look at his wife unclothed during the period each month when the hair grew on her chest and around her breasts, for this would shame her too much and so halt her chances of living some sort of normal married life. And perhaps, Madame Tarentin added, if he allowed her at those times of seclusion to do the drawing and painting she so loved, she would grow reconciled to her deformity and fret about it less.

For several months Pierre Caillou was happy with his new wife. She spoke little, it was true, but he was used to silence, having lived alone for so long, and found her taciturnity a relief rather than a problem. Her stepmother had trained Melusine

17

well: she could cook, sew and clean quite adequately, and she did not complain about the cold and the draughts in the disused classroom they began to use as a bedroom, nor did she nag him for more housekeeping or new clothes. He was able to go on living much as he always had; she did not grudge him the books he sent for from the bookshops in the city, nor the pipes of tobacco he smoked at night when writing up his notes. He knew that she needed greatly to please him, to show her gratitude that he had taken her on, and he argued with himself that this was quite right, for had he not rescued her from a life of miserable loneliness? The villagers might gossip about them for a while, might indulge their curiosity about the new ménage for as long as it took them to become bored with the young couple's obvious blamelessness and contentment, but in time the whispers and sniggers would die down. His neighbours had not, he knew, expected him to marry. He took a certain pleasure in walking with Melusine on Sunday afternoons up and down the village street, and watching the looks cast at his wife's freshly ironed Sunday gown, at her neat coil of red hair under her bonnet, at the scrubbed pair of sabots she kept for best, at her large blue eyes demurely cast down and her wide mouth firmly closed over her sharp little teeth. She was as comely, on these occasions, as any other girl in the village, and he prided himself on the fact that she was also far more intelligent.

He taught her to keep a certain distance. He would not allow her to attend Sunday Mass, for he wanted to wean her from superstition and bigotry, and he did not allow her to climb the hill to visit her parents more than once every two months, for he wanted to give her a chance to lead her own life and become independent of peasant ways. At night she practised reading, writing and spelling under his supervision, and she soon proved herself skilled enough to take dictation, when he needed to think aloud, and to make fair copies into manuscript from his notebooks. Nor did he forget his promise to her parents: when the hair around her breasts came each month he sent her to sleep on his old truckle bed which was set up at these times in the pantry beyond the kitchen at the back of the schoolroom. He let her keep her paints and paper there and retire early, on what he called her red nights, to mess about to her heart's content with water and colours by the light of a tallow candle. After five nights of sleeping separately, she would return, docile and quiet, to his bed, and to any caresses he felt like making. When he asked to see her paintings she looked cross and shook her head at first, but when he threatened to enter her sanctum and fetch them himself she instantly complied. He was surprised at how well this untaught peasant girl could paint, and praised her unstintingly. He spoke to her of the art galleries in the cities he had visited in his days as a student, and her eyes gleamed as she listened. He sent for volumes of engravings, and explained composition to her, and she smiled her rare smile. He knew that he was ignorant of love in the way that his fellow students had practised it, for he had been much too shy to visit brothels with them. He knew that he was ignorant of love in the way that the men in the village practised it, for he suspected them of being animals who treated their wives as holes in the ground to be pissed into and made pregnant year after year. Melusine suited him, for she needed him and looked up to him. So as well as studying her peculiarities he began to love her, and to hope that she loved him in return.

He began to look forward to the evening, to the clock on the mantelpiece chiming seven-thirty, the hour at which he cleared his books off the table and Melusine in her stout calico apron

19

came in to lay the cloth and then brought in the steaming tureen of delicious soup. Afterwards, as she sat sewing in the chair opposite his, or perched next to him at the table and copied out notes under his direction, he would look at her big forehead, her capable square-tipped fingers, her downcast eyes, and want her to look back at him. He began to want to know what went on in her mind.

But she would not respond in the way he wanted. Where he hoped for naïve confidences, for the revelations of her fresh young heart, he got stories she had picked up from her parents as a child, or details of recipes, or gossip overheard on their Sunday walks together. Melusine, it appeared, was not so very different from the other women in the village after all. She was not, after all, original. She told him nothing he could not have heard himself at the baker's or the butcher's or the bar. Even at night, when he lay in her arms after they had made love in the way he liked best, he could not catch her off-guard. She would say she was sleepy, turn over, and hide her eyes from him.

So he began to think about her secret again. It was here, he concluded, that the core of her personality lay. Hadn't he always known that, right from that first day when he caught her drawing in the classroom? So he began to question her, timidly at first and then with growing confidence, about how she felt about the thick growth of hair that came and went every month around her breasts, about how she felt about the stories concerning her mother that were still rife in the village, about how she felt on those nights when she sat in the pantry by the light of her tallow candle and painted the pictures she saw inside herself. Wasn't he right that there were some paintings she never showed him, that she kept secret? But Melusine just looked at him blankly, and shrugged. Or she would kiss him, to quieten him that way. Or, if they were in bed together, she would begin to fondle him in the expert way she had developed. He began to wish she had not learned so well how to please him. Yet he liked being pleased by her, and the more he liked it the more he grew desperate to be sure she loved him and was not just doing her duty.

But the more he pestered her to talk about her secret feelings and thoughts, the more he begged her to show him *all* her paintings, the more Melusine grew silent, irritable and finally rebellious. She said *no* frequently. She kept the key of the pantry door in her pocket. And at the same time he was forced to notice that not only had she developed the habit of littering the kitchen and their bedroom with pictures and drawings and rough sketches, she had also begun to spend more nights shut away from him each month. Five nights at first, then six, then seven, then eight. And the villagers, who liked to pop in and out of the school and see how Melusine and Pierre were getting on, began to notice that Melusine was turning out as undomestic as her mother had been. The villagers began to whisper and giggle about a husband who could not control his eccentric wife. Pierre Caillou, who had always insisted that he didn't care a damn about gossip, began to suffer.

Some days Melusine was late cooking supper, and held a sketch in one hand while she served crisp fried potatoes with the other. Sometimes, on a Sunday, she neglected to put on her pretty clothes and complained she didn't want to take a walk with her husband, she'd rather stay indoors and draw. Often at night now she made love to him in such a brisk perfunctory fashion that he felt used, and that she was rushing the love-making so as to be done with it and sleep.

When, one month, Melusine returned to his bed after nine nights in the pantry, Pierre enquired whether the cause of

her strange behaviour were perhaps that she were pregnant? Melusine laughed: no. Was she ill? Would she see the
doctor? No.

He wondered whether she had taken a lover in secret,
whether she lay in the pantry with some red-faced peasant
and cuckolded him month after month. No, Melusine said.
Laughing at him before she turned away to swill a plate
covered with dried smears of blue and green paint.

He started staying awake at night, so that he could stare
at her as she slept, and try to wrest her secret from her
closed eyelids or the low words she sometimes muttered
as she dreamed. He followed her about the house as she
expertly swept and scrubbed, watching the stoop of her broad
back, the dexterity of her wrists. He tried to trick her in the
evenings, shooting sudden questions at her. He examined the
chest where she kept her clothes mixed up with a rubbish of
dried flowers and chicken feathers and withered chestnuts.
He grew thin with worry, and sometimes forgot to shave in
the mornings. He knew he was behaving strangely, and was
frightened because he had no control over himself any more.
He told Melusine more and more often how much he loved
her, but all she would do was pat him on the arm or cuddle
him as though he were a child seeking reassurance and then
turn away to her housework or her drawing.

On the tenth night of the following month, Melusine had
still not returned to his bed. He lay shaking under the grey
woollen blankets, and tried to put his worry outside himself
so that he could see it and name it and conquer it. Then he
realised that he wasn't simply jealous about his wife's passion
for spending increasing amounts of time away from him locked
in the pantry getting up to unknown mischief. No. He was
deeply concerned for her health and well-being. Here the fear

leapt up and growled at him. His whole body trembled, but he forced himself to go on thinking. If the hair around Melusine's breasts were staying on her body for a longer time each month, did that not logically suggest that there would come a time when his wife would be disfigured by the hair *every* day of *every* month? And supposing the hair went on growing until it had completely covered her body? Had he married a real wild woman of the woods, half-human and half-beast, of the sort the villagers whispered about when telling tales around their fires at night? *Was* she truly a monster, as her parents had hinted?

He leapt up, dragged on his dressing-gown and shoved on his slippers, and went to his office, to the rows of books on his shelves dealing with myth, with anthropology, with fairy stories. With metamorphosis and changelings and werewolves. His fingers ran from index to index, from tome to tome. And he read right through all the notebooks in which for so many years now he had carefully recorded all the superstitions and folkloric customs of the primitive people he lived among.

He lifted his head, surprised by a change in the light. His tallow candle was burning low, and a grey glimmer in the dark sky met his eyes when he pushed open the shutters of the window and leaned out to gulp in the sweet, cold night air. It would soon be dawn. It would soon be breakfast time. Soon, his wife would serenely emerge from her hiding-place and rake out the stove before laying and lighting a fire and boiling a pan of water for coffee.

He walked into the kitchen, and saw that a gold crack of light showed under the pantry door. Then he knew what he had to do. It was very simple. He told himself he was not breaking his promise to Melusine's parents. Things had gone too far for worrying about keeping promises. He had a right

23

to know what his wife got up to night after night on her own in there. He had a right to know whether her chest was still covered with hair after ten nights of seclusion. He had a right to know whether he had unwittingly married a monster.

So he banged on the door. Silence. He rattled the door-knob. Silence. Trying to open the door, he found it was indeed locked. So he knelt down and peered in through the keyhole.

The pantry was ablaze with light. Standing in the centre of the tiny room, leaning one hand on the table, was the most beautiful woman Pierre had ever seen. She was naked. She was tall, and creamy skinned, and her long red hair flowed down her back like streams of fire. There was no blemish anywhere on her. She turned her head and smiled at someone he could not see, someone standing just outside his line of vision. Her lips moved, and she spoke. He could not hear her words, nor could he, squinting, make out their shape by lip-reading. Then she turned her head and looked straight at the door.

He roused the neighbours with his screams. When finally they broke the pantry door down, the candles had been blown out, leaving only the harsh smell of tallow, and there was no one in the room. All Melusine's painting equipment had vanished. On the table there lay only a bundle of red-stained rags.

The footprints in the earth of the flowerbed under the school's pantry window could also be traced in the muddy ruts of the village street. Some people said they stopped at the fishpond. Others said they led towards the river. Still others said they went towards the disused well beside the church. No one could be sure.

As the news of Melusine's disappearance spread, reports

began to come in from neighbouring villages, brought by men and women who had never met her and knew her only as the daughter of Bertrande.

There was a red-haired woman patient in the lunatic asylum at St Rémy. A red-haired woman had been seen boarding the train for Aix. A red-haired prostitute in Marseilles had recently aborted a son with two heads. The painters down from Paris for the summer at Oppède-le-Vieux had a red-haired woman amongst them. There was a red-haired monster lady in the freak show travelling the coast.

None of the villagers could imagine where Melusine had gone.

Dead people go to Purgatory, to have all the badness burnt out of them by a great fire. But the fire happens when you are born, not after you are dead.

We love each other so much. You hold me in your arms, you kiss my breasts, here, here, then you kiss my belly and in between my legs. We will always be faithful to each other. I will hold your hand palm down on the top of the stove until you swear never to leave me.

I kiss and lick all of your skin between your neck and your waist. I am crying because I love you so much. My tears fall on you and are warm on your scars.

When you drink too much I will beat you.

When I drink too much I will beat you.

Now we can have a baby. I am you and you are me. Out of the fire between us comes the baby.

The fire is in the kitchen, its flames leaping high. The mother is in the kitchen, tending the fire and the baby.

I can come into the kitchen to warm myself at the fire as

25

often as I want, and the mother will never turn me away. After I am married I shall keep coming back to the kitchen, to warm myself at her red hands.

Look in the mirror, the mother says, and see how beautiful you are. Silly, you're holding the mirror in the wrong place. Hold it lower down. See the red fire glowing there, in the secret place between your legs. See how beautiful you are. You are like me. You are my daughter. I will love you for ever. You can leave me and you can always come back.

I have branded you with the mark of my love. You are my red baby.

Out of the love between us comes the fire, and the warm kitchen and the mother in the kitchen. Every time we make the fire, we make the kitchen, and the mother.

You can love me, and you can love your mother. You do not have to choose between us.

I shall get married in the kitchen. My mother dropped me in the fire, but she will heal me. She will heal me with her tears.

I shall love you for ever and I shall not beat you.

For my wedding I shall be dressed in red. I shall bring you my red gifts.

I threw my mother in the fire. I shall heal her. I shall heal her, with my tears.

My father and mother love each other so much. I came out of the fire between them. They marry inside me, in the red kitchen.

I take you inside me. I am not afraid of the fire any more. It is inside me. I am in the kitchen. You are there and you do not beat me.

*

Guillaume found he missed his daughter once she was married to Pierre and living down at the bottom of the hill in the schoolhouse. She did not come to Mass and so he never saw her in church. Sometimes on Sundays she walked along the village street with her husband, but she had little enough to say to her parents if she met them. Pierre kept a tight hold on her arm, and Guillaume did not know how to ask her the questions that longed to tumble out of his mouth. He thought perhaps the potato brandy had withered his tongue. The words burned his lips, then died. Sometimes Melusine climbed up the hill to visit her old home, but she sat by the fire in the kitchen gossiping to her stepmother and Guillaume was plainly in the way. Women's talk. He could not enter it, had never known how to. Sometimes he took her little gifts, a basket of eggs or a bunch of freshly picked rosemary or a calf's foot, and she would thank him with a nod and go back to her housework. The words he could not speak swelled in his throat and made it sore.

When Guillaume heard that Melusine was staying longer and longer each month in the pantry, he was persuaded by Madame Tarentin to go down and have a word with her. What word? He knew, but could not say it. She sat silent in front of his silence, and he went away again.

He drank at the bar less than he used to. He stayed at home with his wife and drank potato brandy in the kitchen, Madame Tarentin sitting close by him. They had begun to have a secret. Neither of them spoke of it to the other, but they read of it in each other's eyes. What was happening to Melusine? Would she go the same way as her mother?

On the night of the full moon in November of the year that Melusine disappeared, Guillaume crept out of his bed, down the hill and into the village. He stood underneath the schoolhouse pantry window and tapped at the closed shutters. No chink of light showed, but he knew his daughter was in there. His heart reached through all obstacles, knocking so loudly he knew Melusine must hear it.

She opened the windows, then the shutters, and leaned out in a swift glad movement, her eyes bright, a smile on her lips, her hands coming up in welcome. When she saw her father she drew back, all her delight falling off her like an old shawl.

– Oh, she said: it's you.

Guillaume reached up his hand and patted her arm. She frowned.

– Melusine, he pleaded, making an effort to get the words out of his burning mouth: please let me talk to you.

– Go away, she hissed.

She was dressed only in her nightgown. Tiny pleats flowed from the worn linen yoke. He reached his hands out and tore open the front of the nightgown, then clutched the folds of white linen so that she could not jerk back and escape from him. He saw the red skin, puckered and shiny and ridged, the scars as angry as though she had been dropped in the fire that very day.

– My daughter, he whispered.

Melusine shut her eyes, and turned her head away.

Then Guillaume wept. His tears fell on the scarred skin around his daughter's breasts and flowed on to his hands, warm and stinging. He could not see for weeping. So they remained at the window, the daughter and the father, knotted together by the nightgown, while Guillaume cried.

When he opened his eyes at last, he saw that the skin on his daughter's breast was as creamy and smooth as it had been on the day she was born, and that there was no blemish anywhere on her.

Footnote: I should like to acknowledge, with gratitude, the inspiration of the work of Toni Morrison.

CHARITY

1

I have a young erotic mother. Her hair, shiny and black, curves round her face and flops forward into her large dark eyes. She has an olive skin, olive eyelids, straight black brows. Her mouth is big and wide, her lips plump and rosy as cushions over her large white teeth. Today she's wearing a long dull green mac buttoned down one side and tightly belted around her narrow waist, high-heeled ankle boots, and a red beret, and she's slung her bag diagonally across her front like schoolchildren do.

It's raining. Neither of us has an umbrella, so we walk along arm in arm under the colonnades, up and down, up and down. It's lunchtime. Most people are inside eating. The yellow and grey city seems empty. Except for us. Talking as we pace, exchanging stories as fast as we can. Months since we've seen each other, so many words to turn over in our hands and offer each other like pieces of new bread torn off the still warm loaf. Then she makes up her mind, and invites me home.

We shake ourselves in the hallway like two wet dogs. She pulls me after her into the bedroom to find me some dry clothes. We watch each other undress. Slither of a rose-coloured slip, of seamed black stockings. She turns back the blue quilt on the bed, and I slide in next to her. My mother's flesh is warm. The sheets are cool and smooth. I lay my hands on her hips and pull her close, kiss her soft mouth, her shoulders, stroke her hair, the wet silky place between her legs. The storm drums on the roof. She kisses and caresses me. Her smell grows stronger, like a garden after the rain. She offers me her breast, round and white and fat, ardently we lie in each other's arms, touching kissing sucking biting, then my swollen cunt boils over and I come.

I wake up from this dream disconcerted, still fizzing. I'll tell it to Gabriella tomorrow when we're having breakfast together at my kitchen table, and she'll laugh. She'll be dipping a sweet biscuit into her little cup of black coffee, her feet tucked up under her, comfortable amongst the cushions of the basket chair, her profile alert against the white wall, and then she'll light a cigarette, impatient to tell me *her* dream. Her presence unleashes our words. We're off. Each time we see one another, this jostling at the start, glad galloping down the track of stories. After knowing her for twenty years.

2

Auntie's kitchen smelt of the damp washing which we hung on a pulley above the fireplace and on racks in front of it. Our woollen jumpers, the sheets and towels, made a moist tent over our heads. The floor was brown lino, bruised and dull. The sink and draining-board were tin. We had a cupboard for food and crockery, a tea-trolley on which we kept the iron and the radio, and a table at which we ate, read, played cards, filled in the football coupon. It was a crowded place, things everywhere: saucers full of cigarette stubs and ashes, piles of old magazines, piles of clothes ready for ironing, our wellingtons stood against the back door and our two bicycles leaned against the wall nearby. We didn't have a garden shed so we kept the spade and rake in a corner, together with a sack of compost and a pile of wooden seed-trays.

The kitchen was dark, as though it was always winter. We had a standard lamp with a flowered shade that stuck out like a skirt, and a smaller lamp on the table for reading by. Auntie was a great reader, starting with the morning paper and going on to the magazines people gave her, Whitaker's *Almanack*, a dog-eared gardening book, and crime novels from the library. When it rained we set a bucket to catch the drips. We were quite cosy, jammed up together by the fire, Auntie in her chair with an ashtray balanced on the worn arm, the dog on her feet, and me on the old leather pouffe holding the toasting-fork. Sometimes we had toast with pork dripping for tea, if it was a Monday. The best was sausages, which Auntie taught me to fry over the open fire. There was a perfectly good cooker in the corner, but we both preferred this sort of cooking, like camping. The sausages were beef, tight and shiny they rolled in their spluttering fat. We liked them black and charred, then we clapped them between thick slices of bread and butter. The softness of the white bread, the heat of the sausage melting the butter to gold puddles that dripped down my chin, swallows of warm tea alternating with bites of sausage sandwich, this was a banquet. The dog got the crusts.

The little estate of council houses near the railway line was built to look like cottages grouped around a central green. Low brick houses, with plain front doors with little wooden porches over them, plain windows with white sashes and sills. Built in the twenties I think. Cramped inside, but not ugly to look at, not like the modern blocks and high-rises, and, out the back, gardens that ran gaily into one another, separated only by low withy fences. At the bottom of the gardens was the railway line. Auntie showed me how to leave pennies on the track for the trains to flatten. Sometimes they struck sparks. That was the best route home from primary school, along the little embankment thick with rose bay willow herb and cow parsley. I learned the names in nature study. It was my wild place. I could lie hidden in the long grass, its purple fringes waving above my head, and stare at the sky and listen out for the trains. If it was raining or snowing I came home the short way, by the road, and Auntie would hang my socks and gloves to dry in front of the fire and let me have hot Marmite.

Auntie was not what you would call a goodlooking woman most of the time, except in the afternoons when she got tidied up for her visitors. She was tall, with a jaunty face. She didn't look anything like the other children's mothers, the ones who waited for them outside the playground railings and wore bunchy blouses and full flowered skirts. Auntie wore men's jeans, thick and straight, in heavy indigo, big sweaters. She put her hair up, morning and night, into a turban, and brushed it down in the afternoons when she put on a frock. She always wore bright red lipstick and could talk with a cigarette in her mouth. Sometimes she seemed very old to me, and sometimes more like a boy. She let me play with her curlers, pierced metal cylinders with loops of black elastic, and with her big wrinkled hairpins. One of my treats, when I'd been good, was going into her handbag to see what she'd got, another was helping her wash her hair in the bath, carefully tipping jugs of water over her head until she was done.

That was the same jug Auntie used for me when I had colds: enamel, with stains inside. She put a brown capsule, thick and squashy, in the bottom, then covered it with boiling water. I sat by the fire with a towel over my head and inhaled the steam of the melted capsule, so rich and hot I almost choked. Then she made me go to bed early with Vick rubbed on my chest and a mug of hot orange. She made me take cod-liver oil and halibut-liver oil and gave me boiled sweets afterwards as a reward. My other great reward for being good was being allowed to go by myself to children's cinema on Saturday morning, with threepence extra for a bag of chips on the way home. Being good meant not getting home from school until four o'clock every day in the week, by which time the last of the visitors would have gone and Auntie would be putting the kettle on for tea. Nor was I allowed to disturb Auntie early on weekend mornings. We never had dinner on Saturdays and I liked this. I was free to eat my chips while dawdling along the High Street, and then to play alone all afternoon on the embankment. Auntie would come from the pub, have her sleep, and then we'd have tea together and listen to the radio.

Before she went to the pub Auntie would do the shopping in the market. Tea on Saturday was always a good one. We both loved fried potatoes with onions. Or we'd have a rasher of

bacon, or mushrooms on toast, or sausages. I always made the
cocoa last thing, she said I made cocoa better than anyone. If it
was a weekday I had to polish my shoes ready for the morning,
then I'd read comics or a book in bed until she came in to turn
the light off. Have you said your prayers, she'd ask. And I'd
say yes. Then she'd pull the blankets up round my ears, kiss
me, and go. Her kiss tasted of cigarettes. If I had a nightmare
or if I couldn't go to sleep she let me come and sleep in her
bed. It sagged a bit. We slept together in the dip in the middle.
Under the thick warmth of her pyjamas she was both bony
and soft. I'd wriggle to get into a good position, she'd grunt
at me to quieten down, she smelt of face cream. She didn't put
her curlers in till the morning, she said they hurt too much
to sleep in.

She was a mixture of easygoing and strict. I could fiddle
about in her make-up drawer, or the box of old clothes she
kept for dressing-up, or her envelope of photos of when she
was young, and as long as I didn't break anything through
carelessness she didn't mind. When I was small she perched
me on the crossbar in front of her on her bike and rode me
round and round the little green at the front of the houses.
Then she taught me to ride my own bike. She got me some
roller-skates from a jumble sale, with small metal wheels and
worn leather straps, and waved me off. But she didn't much
like me mixing with other children and never let me bring a
friend home to tea. I went to other children's houses for tea
at first at primary school, then less and less because I couldn't
invite them back. We'll keep ourselves to ourselves, she always
said. She took me to Mass on Sunday evenings, and we sat
at the back. Once when the priest came to visit she slammed
the door in his face. The first and only time I forgot not to
come home straight from school and walked into the house

without knocking and went to find her in her bedroom she yelled at me and threw me out. When she came to find me she slapped me. She was very firm about washing hands after the toilet, please and thank you, things like that. But she didn't mind me getting filthy in the garden digging in the patch she gave me next to the sweet peas, or trying to cut my own hair like I did one time, or repeating the rude words and rhymes I learned in the playground. When she laughed it was a hoarse sound because of all the cigarettes. When she washed my hair for me in the bath she made it stick up stiff in a soapy spike before she rinsed it with the jug. If I didn't cry with the soap in my eyes I got a boiled sweet, then I'd sit on her lap by the fire until my hair was dry and she would talk. About winning on the Premium Bonds or on the pools, or the Grand National. We placed our racing bets through the milkman, but we never won anything.

There was an old clock on the mantelpiece, with a soft regular tick. When it chimed, Auntie always exclaimed: ten o'clock struck at the castle gate! If I disagreed with her about anything she would retort: what, girl, you dare to thwart me thus? Me making a noise was a schemozzle, a mess was a pile of tack, me complaining was a performance. Twelve noon was the sun going over the yard arm and meant you could have a drink. A suit on a woman was a costume. She said I kept my eyes in my stomach and that enough was as good as a feast. When she burped she said *pardon*. I loved the way she smoked, moistening her cigarette in the corner of her mouth between her red lips or holding it between her thumb and forefinger. She kept her cigarettes in a little silver metal case, held down by an elastic, like a row of babies in bed, and she had a silvery lighter she showed me how to fill with petrol. Strike a light, darling, she would say, holding up her cigarette, and I would rush to light it for her. She could blow perfect smoke rings, she said she learned how in the army.

It didn't occur to me to question her much about her life before I lived with her. Not until I was forced to become aware, through other children's gibes and rhymes, that she was odd and therefore bad and so I too because I lived with her. She had a brother and sisters, she told me once, all older than her, all emigrated now to Canada and New Zealand. One died of scarlet fever when he was little. A long time ago, well before the war. Then she'd give me a shove: stir a stump. And I'd get off her lap and make the cocoa with the half-pint of milk carefully saved from teatime. By now the fire would be sunk to a low red mass. Auntie would consider it, frowning as she made her decision, then tip on just a few more coals. To any further questions on my part she'd retort: what you don't know can't hurt you. And that was that.

3

Who made you?
God made me.
Why did God make you?
To know, love and serve Him in this life, and to be happy ever after with Him in the next.

Those are the words printed in the books in front of us on our desks. We know them by heart. It's hard to believe God made us, really, because we can't see Him. Whereas everywhere in the school we've got statues of the Virgin Mary in different outfits. She's far more real. Our nuns belong to the Order of Our Lady of Perpetual Succour. Sister Boniface, known as Ugly Face because of her mole and her moustache, has explained to us many times that perpetual means everlasting, never-failing, while succour is a form of the virtue of charity and means giving and sustaining. The words are written up all over the school in curly script, in here too, over the blackboard behind Ugly Face on a sort of gold banner. Alice, sitting just in front of me, raises her head to look at them, then whispers loudly to Mary, her neighbour: perpetual suck; perfect sucker; and they bend giggly faces over their catechisms.

Ugly Face has been repotting the spider plants she grows on the high tiled windowsills of our classroom. She's forgotten to take off her gardening apron, thick blue cotton tied around her waist with blue strings. The colour of Our Lady's robe, the colour of Nivea Creme tins and the little salt wrappers in packets of crisps. Sitting at her desk like a pulpit she picks earth from under her fingernails while she drones us through our little books. God has no colour because He's an invisible spirit, but everything connected with Our Lady is blue.

Next month, in May, Our Lady's month, we shall be received, those of us holy enough, into the Children of Mary. So far we've been Agnesians, with red ribbon sashes tied diagonally over our gymslips, and gold medals, showing St Agnes and her lamb of purity, slung on red cords around our necks. We wear these to school Mass and to Benediction on Friday afternoons. St Agnes is suitable for us because she died very young. Our Lady didn't die in the normal way. She fell asleep in the arms of St John, then angels came with a silver tray and carried her up to heaven on it. Now she sits side by side with Our Lord on a throne, they look exactly the same age. When you're a Child of Mary you get a blue sash and walk at the front of the May procession, you lead the recitation of the Rosary at lunchtimes during novenas, and you kneel on the special prie-dieux set up in the aisle next to the nuns praying in shifts for round the clock perpetual adoration of the Blessed Sacrament in June, just before the feast of Corpus Christi.

Perpetual blessed suck, Alice whispers. Her mouth nuzzles at the words. Mary goes red in the face and coughs. Miss Barney, the biology mistress, complains girls of our age are awful, always whispering and giggling. She's trying to teach us to be good citizens who'll go on to be teachers and lawyers and doctors and she gets so cross when we go into fits during her lessons when she says words like breast. She was teaching us respiration and she said: you can feel your heart beating, it's just under your left breast. We all laughed, we were so ashamed she should use such words. Also she asked us how many entrances there were into our bodies and none of us knew. She was shocked. But she's a Protestant so she doesn't count.

Mary and Alice and I all chose desks together at the start of this term. Mary's been my best friend up till now, but I'm thinking of asking Alice to be instead. Alice is friends with me but she's friends with the bad girls too, the ones like Karen and Janice who know the name of the sin St Maria Goretti died rather than commit. A boy stabbed her with a knife because she wouldn't do it. I don't know what it was. The bad girls, Karen and Janice and the others, they talk about things like this in corners, then they look at me and laugh. They whip off their hats the minute they're through the school gates and unbutton their macs, they eat sweets on the street and wear nylons at weekends when the nuns can't see them. They talk to boys too, the black-blazered ones from Haberdashers up the road with long grey flannel legs and broken voices and spots.

This term I've been made form captain. That means having to keep everyone quiet before morning and afternoon assembly and in between classes and when we line up for dinner. The bad girls make a row and I have to report them. They hate me and laugh at me, it makes me very unhappy. Anyway, it's lower-class to be bad. Alice doesn't understand that because her parents are foreigners, her grandparents didn't come to England until the start of the First World War. Alice has got hairs under her arms and at the top of her legs. So have I. Once when I was staying the weekend at her house she pulled out one of her hairs in the bathroom and then showed it to me in the bedroom. It was long and black and curly. Mine are pale. I didn't dare show her one. She laughed at me. That Saturday her mother took me to buy a bra, she said I needed a proper one. The little draper's in Golders Green was dark and hot and smelled of scent. The Jewish lady assistant came into the cubicle with a handful of bras and actually touched me. Bend forwards from the waist, dear, she said: bend into it from the waist. She put her hands on my bosoms and pulled them up so they fitted. Very nice dear, she said: very nice.

Ugly Face gets bored listening to us recite the answers from the catechism. I watch her gaze wander over our desks, each one with its sloping wooden lid, inset china inkwell. Like the little houses in packed rows, all the same, down the hill where Mary lives. We're not really all the same of course. Mary's parents are quite poor but definitely not lower-class. They don't have to pay fees for Mary because she's so bright, she won a scholarship after she passed the eleven-plus. On the other hand there are girls here whose parents are rich enough to pay the fees but lower-class. Lots of money but badly educated. That's why they want their daughters to have a good education. You don't have to pass the eleven-plus to get in here, you just have to pass the entrance exam and be able to pay the fees. I got a scholarship too, like Mary.

The bad girls are lower-class of course, but some of the good ones are as well. You can tell by the pictures they paste on the underneath of their desk lids: highly coloured pictures of the Sacred Heart, big soppy birthday cards of pink kittens and puppies. They're the ones who wear scapulars under their blouses, and cords jangling with tin miraculous medals, all identical. I've got a real Italian mantilla, black lace, that Mary's mother gave me when she came back from holiday, and I've got a picture of Our Lady feeding Jesus stuck under my desk lid. It's from the Middle Ages so it's not rude. Modern pictures of women with bare bosoms are rude, that's why Mary's father hides his at the bottom of the wardrobe where he thinks no one will find them. But we found them that time when we were playing Sardines. I've also got postcards of women dancing in fields by an Italian artist called Botticelli, okayed by Ugly Face because they're art.

Not all art is OK. Sister Wilfred the librarian has pasted little black strips of paper over the rude bits of naked men in the Greek art books. She lets Alice and me use the library because we don't make a noise. We're doing a project on Charity this term in RE and we have to do research. We found a book with pictures of the Virtues, who were women from olden times. Justice had a pair of scales, Faith had a sword. Charity was a lady with no clothes on her top under the black bit of paper, feeding four babies at once. I saw a lady do that once in the dentist's waiting-room. She pulled up her jumper, quick as a flash, and I saw her floppy white chest before she pressed the baby's head to it. The waiting-room was small, with a high ceiling and a gas fire. It was gloomy and dark. It was cold, it smelled of leather and dust and gas. I was sitting there praying the drill wouldn't hurt too much and thinking about what the martyrs had to go through and there was that lady with a bare fat chest. All year long I dread the next visit to the dentist and the terrible pain, it's never out of my mind. The minute it's over I start dreading the next time. The drill grinds away, slow and noisy, and you wait for when it will go on a nerve and make you want to scream. I don't scream. I bear it for the holy souls in Purgatory. The lady's baby screamed and she pulled up her jumper just as though she was in her own home. The Virgin Mary on my desk lid isn't like that. She's far more beautiful than the stupid plaster statues all round the school. When I'm crying my eyes out she's the one I pray to. She knows how much I wish I was thin and popular and pretty with long straight hair and not so clever. She understands all this and she still loves me. She knows why I'm praying so hard the bell will ring soon for the end of school. Before Janice and Karen can say anything.

The classroom windows, high up so that we can't see out of them, are open on both sides. Warm air drifts in, the whine of the gardener's lawn-mower, the smell of cut grass, the buzz of bees, the drone of an invisible aeroplane. Next to the spider plants are several jam-jars filled with pink blotting paper and sprouting broad beans, a pot of cacti, a little statue of St Joseph. On the wall, held up by a wooden bracket and surrounded by glass vases of forget-me-nots Ugly Face puts there twice a week, is a statue of Our Lady of Perpetual Succour. She has long fair hair and outstretched arms and a gold crown. She wears a cloak, and under it she shelters a lot of children. Mary's mother says such statues are in bad taste and won't have them in the house, plaster is lower-class. She's got a little china one of the Mother and Child, white with gold flecks, that she picked up at the church jumble sale for half a crown because the ladies running the white elephant stall didn't know its value. They're the ones who clean the parish church every

week. Mary's mother does the flowers. The other ladies don't
know how to do them. We only have to clean the church once
a month, it's part of our Girl Guides community service. I like
digging the old stumps of candle wax out of the iron holders
with my penknife, it's really violent. I hate the parish church.
It's like a cathedral, but small. The walls are pale blue, and
behind the altar there's an enormous painting on the wall with
all the saints standing on the steps going up to heaven. It's too
bright, it's ugly. Once Mary's mother was giving Father Dean's
housekeeper a hand with the spring cleaning and she found the
dustbin was full of empty whisky bottles. She brought them
home so that the dustmen wouldn't be scandalised. Only the
parish ladies know, not the men. They do jobs like weeding the
flowerbeds outside the church sometimes. But mostly they are
in the Knights of St Columba and run things, like the bazaar
and the fête, the parish outing and the pilgrimage.

The sunshine is like polish on the red tiled floor that the
postulants have to wash every week. The postulants have
to help the lay sisters with all the heavy housework round
the school as a test of their vocations, then some of them,
once they're through the novitiate, go on to Catholic teacher
training college up in London, and the others become lay
sisters. Sometimes the postulants get the laundry muddled
up and send us back nuns' bras, huge and loose and floppy. I
know a lot about nuns' lives partly because of being a boarder
and being closer to them than the daygirls are, partly because
of reading all the books in the cupboard at the back of the
classroom. Lives of the saints. Most of the women saints were
nuns. You can't really be a saint if you have a husband. Ugly
Face hopes that some of us, once we're in the Children of
Mary, will develop religious vocations and join the Order.
The best and highest thing a girl can do is become a nun,

44

but if she hasn't been called by God then she'll become a wife and mother. It's not so high, but it's what most girls end up doing when they leave.

Ex-pupils come back as Old Girls to Parents' Day and the Christmas bazaar. Alice's mother is the most stylish. She wears chiffon and silk, big hats, and she has red fingernails. She has a curvy figure and good legs and a crocodile handbag. She told Alice she still makes love with Alice's father, at least once a week. When I go to tea there we have bagels and cream cheese, black bread and gherkins. Once we had pickled herring and another time smoked salmon. Alice's house is full of thick white carpets, armchairs covered in gold plush, cabinets that light up full of grey and blue figurines of ladies dancing, big oil paintings, very modern.

Modern art is so easy, a child could do it. I told this to Miss van Doren one day in art class. She was very cross because Sister Agatha had come in to say we had to learn to do religious painting and Miss van Doren shouted at her that you could make a picture of a watering-can religious if you felt that way. Then she shouted at me: go on then, do some abstract art and show me how easy it is. I didn't know where to put the lines. I prefer doing my pictures of ladies in costume, Tudor or Victorian. Miss van Doren said I should draw them nude first and then put the clothes on them but I can't do that. For a long time I couldn't draw hands, the ladies' arms just ended in points. Alice's father laughed at them, mice he called them. Now I can do proper hands, and eyelashes as well. Alice mucks about in art class, flicking paint and so on. I never do, because art is my best subject.

Alice is Jewish but her parents think a convent education can't harm a young girl. All the other schools in the area are either Protestant or secondary moderns. We do elocution and deportment as well as all the other subjects, and next year we'll start ballroom dancing with Sister Agatha. For deportment we have to walk round the hall with books on our heads and curtsy to Ugly Face without dropping them. Then she inspects our fingernails and our white gloves. Last summer we had to kneel on the floor and she measured down from the hem of our tennis dresses to make sure that they were not too short. Two inches above the floor was all right but no more. Alice sits in on religious education and comes to Mass and Benediction, she's in the choir too, but of course she can't become a Child of Mary. Or a nun. The girls who become nuns have a wedding-day after they've been postulants for six months, then they die to the world. It's very beautiful and sad. They glide up the aisle in their white dresses with their hair spread out down their backs, then the habit and veil are fitted over them and they disappear.

But if you get married and have children you disappear as well. Housewives stay at home all day and talk about recipes and babies, they read women's magazines, they go to the hairdresser's every week and have their hair cut off and have perms. I shall never get married and have children. I might try and go to university, but after that I'm going to become a nun. I shall take a vow of silence and never speak. When the time comes I'll just do it. I wouldn't dream of telling Father Dean. It's bad enough having to go to confession to him and have him call me by my name when he gives me my penance. I'd never tell him what I thought about anything. I tell him the same sins every week, quarrelling with my schoolfriends and talking in the cloakroom, and he always gives me three Hail Marys.

Father Dean doesn't like the nuns much. He calls them the holy hens. He said that last time he came to dinner at Mary's house, one weekend when I was staying. He laughed, and put out his glass for more wine. Mary's mother had made egg and bacon tart but she told Father Dean it was called Quiche Lorraine. She had put a lace cloth and candles on the table and was wearing her best dress and Mary's father was wearing the suit he puts on when he goes to the Knights of St Columba. Mary's mother laughed at everything Father Dean said. I don't think a married woman should behave like that. It's not fair on Mary's father. She says he works so hard that when he comes home every night he falls asleep in front of the fire and never speaks. He doesn't make much money. He says it's the Jews' fault, coming into the country and taking all the good jobs. Once he said that in front of Alice when we were both there for Sunday lunch. Mary's mother went very red and so did Alice. They both started talking at once so Mary's father carried on, about how lucky we are to be English because the English are the best and what a good thing it is there aren't any coloured people in the Knights of St Columba.

Our nuns have schools in Africa, to educate the coloured people and get them to become Christians. We save up our pocket money for the babies to be baptised. Also we pray for the Communists, and all the poor people behind the Iron Curtain. The Communists kill unborn babies. At school there are two Nigerian girls in the sixth form, and several girls from Hong Kong. When their parents come to Speech Day everyone always treats them especially nicely to show them they're just as good as us. Once when I was with Mary and her parents we had to drive through the East End. There were lots of coloured people standing around in the street. The women were all in party frocks in very bright colours, red and pink together. I felt queer looking at them, they were not like anybody's mother that I know. Here you never see women standing in

47

doorways holding babies and chatting. The babies are always in prams in the front garden and the mothers only go out for shopping. Mary's father says all the Jews used to live in the East End, but now the coloured people do. Nowadays the Jews live in the same neighbourhood as Mary's family. Once the coloured people start moving in as well Mary's family will move somewhere else.

Ugly Face closes her catechism with a snap. As well as her blue gardening apron she's still wearing her blue over-sleeves, heavy cotton gathered at wrist and elbow. Arms folded in front of her now, hands clasped, blue eyes burning in her white face under their heavy black brows that almost meet. She looks very young, she's got a really peaceful face. Mary's mother says nuns look so young because of their sheltered lives with no responsibilities. By that she means her own work of running the house and bringing up her children and giving piano and dancing lessons. Ugly Face is sorry for Mary's mother because she has to go out to work and can't dedicate her entire life to her family like other girls' mothers do. Only lower-class mothers work. Mary's mother isn't lower-class of course. Ugly Face said we should be charitable. Some women had to work for the good of their families and we shouldn't judge them. They had to get up extra early in the mornings to clean the grates and light the fires and get the children's breakfast. Mary put her hand up and said that her mother didn't do that, she lay in bed with a cup of tea.

In her own way Ugly Face isn't bad. Like now, in her blue gardening apron, when she leans forward with flashing eyes telling us about charity, which means perfect love. Mary's father says that in some countries, like he saw in the war, they think moustaches on women are attractive. That was how he met Mary's mother, in Italy in the war. She came back to England with him and they got married. He became a Catholic to please her and now he's really keen on it, he's Secretary of the Knights of St Columba and he organises all the parish trips. Ugly Face's moustache is just a thin line above her upper lip. Mary's father noticed it at the school bazaar when he was helping her pack the bran tub. I watched him talking to her, teasing her until she went red and burst out laughing. He was treating her like he treats all us girls. He's quite handsome, Mary's father, with wavy black hair and a little black moustache. Nuns aren't supposed to be like women but Ugly Face is. Moles, too, Mary's father said, are not unattractive.

Mary's mother was beautiful when she was young, you can see that from the photographs. She says having six children has ruined her figure. Her black hair has a bit of silver in it, at the front, and she wears it in a low bun behind, like a ballerina. She always wears lipstick. She puts it on after lunch, thick and red, and she re-powders her nose, she uses the little mirror of the powder compact from her handbag. I hate women doing that in public, they should do it in secret. But I like seeing the inside of the handbag. And its perfumey smell. Mary's mother can't afford nice clothes though. She makes the children's clothes on her machine and she buys her own clothes from Marks and Spencer. She tries to do things the English way, because Mary's father hates all foreigners except for her, but she's still got a strong Italian accent, especially when she's angry. Foreign food is very oily and greasy but Mary's mother is a really good cook. She says they don't have tinned spaghetti on toast in Italy. She's learned how to cook English food and she's really quite good at it. She can do carrots in white sauce, cauliflower cheese, steak and kidney pudding, scones, lots of things.

That day when they were talking about Ugly Face and whether she was attractive or not I was there for high tea. High tea is lower-class but Mary's father likes it. We were having cold ham and lettuce, beetroot, spring onions, tomatoes and chutney. We have salad cream on our salad and Mary's mother has olive oil, she's not allowed to pour it all over everyone's lettuce, only on her own plate. It was all served in little glass dishes that fit into a round wooden tray. When they bring people back from High Mass for drinks before Sunday lunch Mary's mother fills it with peanuts, cocktail olives, cheese balls and twiglets. Mary and I have to keep offering it round while the grown-ups have gin and tonic and cigarettes. Then we have to lay the table for lunch and wash up afterwards. It's very boring, so I offer it up for the holy souls in Purgatory. I only hope someone will do the same for me when I am dead. Mary's mother said how sorry she was for Ugly Face, denied her natural fulfilment and knowing nothing of real life. That was after Mary's father said that about women with moustaches. In England you buy olive oil at the chemist's, it's used for earache. After tea we had to do the washing-up again. The saints had to put up with things like that. The Little Flower had to work in the laundry with a nun who kept splashing her. She offered it all up. It's called the Little Way. It's one of the hardest roads to holiness. Sometimes I think that after I've left university I might put off being a nun for a bit. Alice and Mary and I want to live in London and be bohemians and meet beatniks. So I might put it off.

When I'm staying at Mary's house I can play with her dolls. The best one is Anya. She's got long blonde hair and blue eyes and she's very slim. Mary's garden is quite big, because they're on a corner, it goes round the house on three sides. At the back there's a little sunken lawn with trellises of fruit trees and long thin beds underneath them filled with marigolds and nasturtiums and forget-me-nots. There's a gap in the low brick wall holding up the trees and flowerbeds, it's Anya's cave. She gets kidnapped by brigands and kept in the cave, they take all her clothes away and just leave her covered with a rug. She's very brave but she can't escape. The brigand chief says to her that she's his favourite slave. He takes the rug off her and looks at her with no clothes on for a long time. He stares at her breasts. Very quietly he tells her that she's got the most beautiful breasts he's ever seen.

Another of my favourite places is under the soft fruit bushes, under the black netting. You can wriggle in to the far end and it's a completely secret place, black earth and grass and weeds and the raspberry bushes meeting overhead. Anya gets lost in the forest. She's in medieval times, she's run away from her parents' castle dressed as a boy, she's following the robbers' army. She's supposed to hate the robber chief but secretly she's in love with him. He finds her in the forest and makes her his page. Then she has to sleep in his tent. One night he discovers she's not a boy after all but a woman. He sees her with no clothes on, with her top all bare. That's one of my favourite stories. I play it over and over again. Nobody else knows about it except Mary, most girls think dolls are for playing mothers and babies. Grown-ups are stupid. They can't remember what it's like to be my age. I've sworn to myself I'll never forget what it's like to be ten, and now eleven. I don't know why.

I don't remember my parents. Auntie told me they died in a plane crash when I was two, coming back from holiday. I was lucky they left me with my aunt or I'd have been dead too. I don't miss them at all because I can't remember them. I'm very lucky because first of all Auntie adopted me, then when I got too much for her the nuns let me be a full-time boarder. They want to give me the best possible chance. In olden times orphans had to live in the workhouse and were dependent on charity, the same as the African children are dependent on us nowadays. Charity means people giving their loose change. Catholic orphans had the worst time because the English hated Catholics and didn't want them to get good jobs. The Foundress started the Sisters of Our Lady of Perpetual Succour especially to care for the Catholic girls and their babies, her nuns rescued them and put them into their orphanages. They brought them up to be good Catholics and not to be afraid, they got some of them fostered or adopted in good Catholic homes, and they looked after the rest of them in the orphanages. Some of the orphans had mothers but the mothers knew it was in the children's best interests to leave them with the nuns so that they could find jobs and make a fresh start.

Being illegitimate is the worst thing you can be. Another word for it is bastard. It means you haven't got a father and that your mother isn't married and that she did something really terrible and lower-class. It is very shocking and dirty. It's like an extra dose of original sin and it never rubs off. People whisper and point when they see an illegitimate person. Janice and Karen said I was but it isn't true.

Ugly Face is walking up and down by the blackboard now, her hands wrapped in her blue apron. All the nuns walk like that, with their hands out of sight under their scapulars. I tried it, it's quite comfortable. I've also tried the effect of a nun's veil. I do it with a bath towel. But my face is so plump. I wish I had dark eyes and high cheekbones, then a veil might really suit me. Ugly Face is talking about history now. She's saying we shouldn't celebrate Bonfire Night because it's an anti-Catholic feast, it's about burning Catholics. Guy Fawkes was a Catholic. When you burn the guy you're burning a Catholic.

Mary's father lets them have fireworks though, because he wasn't a Catholic until he grew up and he loves letting off rockets. He hates the Irish even though so many of them are Catholics. Mary's mother says Irish Catholics are different from Italian Catholics, the Pope is always Italian. Ugly Face says the Irish are best and that we should pray for the Jews and the Protestants and the pagans to be converted to the One True Faith. I'm very lucky I was born here and that I'm English. It must be terrible to be born abroad and be a foreigner. All the foreigners try and come to this country because it's the best. Ugly Face's parents sailed to Liverpool because there were no jobs in Ireland and the people were starving. Some of Mary's mother's relatives came here too, because they were so poor in the south of Italy.

Very soon I should think the bell will ring for the end of afternoon school. I hope it does, so that there's no time for the question and answer session. Janice and Karen have told me what question they're going to ask and I'm praying the bell will go before they've got a chance to say it. I'm praying to Our Lady not to let me down.

The classroom has its own special smell, chalkdust and polish. It's like being on a ship, sailing along high above the garden, we're so high up, on the third floor, with the air blowing through. Sometimes at school I'm very happy, like when we're all sitting quietly reading our set book and no one's torturing me. Last summer, my first year here, we had some of our lessons outside, sitting in a circle on the grass. The big lawn has oak trees on it, with benches. That's the only part we're allowed in, except for the tennis courts below. Further down is a sort of wild part, with very long grass, and a pond, and a little path winding in and out of the trees, and a hut with a statue of Our Lady. I went down there once with Mary and Alice, it was private and hidden, like being under the raspberry bushes, only even better because it was forbidden. We lay in the grass and told secrets.

Far away on one side of the lawn is the nuns' cemetery, with white crosses and rose bushes. Far away on the other side is the convent proper, the part we can never go into. At the back of it are three arches which give on to the nuns' part of the garden, and sometimes you can see the novices walking up and down there with the novice mistress in their white veils. We're not supposed to look at them.

The nuns also have a walled kitchen garden. Once, for a dare, I looked through the door in the wall to see what it was like. There were rows of cabbages and leeks in square plots, with narrow paths between them, and there were fruit trees trained round the walls. There were beehives in one corner, and a compost heap, and sweet peas. It was so peaceful and quiet. One of the lay sisters was digging. She looked up and saw me so I ran away, but she couldn't get me into trouble because she didn't know my name. We're not allowed to talk to the lay sisters.

The thing about the convent that really fascinates me is all the places we're not allowed. I long and long to know what it's like inside the nuns' part. It's there, so close you can touch it, but you can't go in. You can't see what it's like. It's dark, and invisible, you can only imagine it. It's a secret house side by side with the one you know, like in the story when the girl walks through the mirror into the world behind it. The daygirls' houses are ordinary sized and modern, with lots of windows and no dark places or secret places. When I'm staying with Mary and Alice we can go wherever we want in them. We know them inside out. There aren't any surprises. Whereas the convent is over a hundred and fifty years old, the main bit. You come into the round entrance hall, it's all white pillars and a carved white fireplace and pictures on the ceiling. Opposite is the library, done by a decorator called Adam, with another big white fireplace and more pillars. To the left is the Red Passage, dark and low with red tiles on the floor, which leads to the school part, and on the right is a narrow black corridor, more like a tunnel really, which leads through into the cloister. We turn right into the cloister and get into chapel, into the main part. We're not allowed to turn left, because that's the nuns' cloister, it goes into the convent. More than anything I want to be able to walk around that corner and see what's there. But of course I can't. It's completely impossible. It's a forbidden place. So there's this whole half of the building I'll never be able to see inside. Not unless I become a nun. We're only allowed through the white entrance hall on the way to the chapel. There's a separate entrance for the school, in the big yard, that leads straight into the cloakrooms. I often pay a visit to the Blessed Sacrament at lunchtime so that I can go down the black tunnel and along the cloister.

Ugly Face says the nuns' food is much worse than ours, she says we're lucky to get such food. We find that hard to believe. We get thin grey meat full of gristle and fat, carrot dice tasting of soap, watery cabbage, lettuce with no salad cream. The chips are best, we get those on Fridays with fried fish which is mostly thick batter. When we have blancmange, which is white and wobbly with a glacé cherry on top, the big girls call it an Agatha. They laugh quietly so Sister Agatha won't hear. St Agatha was a martyr who had her bosoms torn off. When it's your turn to be a server you eat after everybody else and you get more food, the kitchen nuns keep it back for you. At table the big girls serve out the food and always give themselves the most. We're not allowed to talk until Sister Agatha rings her little bell, and it's like waiting in the mornings for assembly to begin, it's almost impossible not to talk. Then you have to stand up and own up to talking and everyone looks at you. If you stand up too often you get sent to Sister Superior. She has a terrifying face, white, like a cat's, she has gimlet eyes and a cold quiet voice. Getting sent to see her in her office is the worst thing that can happen to you, apart from being expelled. Two of the boarders got expelled last term, they were found in bed together. I didn't understand why that was so disgusting, Karen and Janice were giggling about it in class, those two girls did something we aren't supposed to know about. I wish I knew what it was. Alice and Mary both knew but they wouldn't tell me.

Another disgusting thing that happened was to Mademoiselle, she went for a walk in the far end of the park that's next to the school, and a man attacked her. He jumped out of the bushes on to her, she pleaded with him not to, then she ran away. Sister Agatha told us about it at morning assembly. She was very upset about what all the parents would think and said we must never go for walks in the park by ourselves, especially not down the far end. We always have to stay in full view of whoever's taking recreation. It always used to be Sister Matthew. She left soon after she was professed, she went off to the Poor Clares, which is a much stricter order. They sleep sitting up on bare boards with all their clothes on and they never speak. They are real contemplatives. Sister Matthew always walked around as though she was in a trance, with a dreamy expression on her face. She wasn't much good at keeping us in order. At first she took us for RE. But Karen and Janice, and Pearl, one of the girls from Hong Kong, started to torture her by asking her questions she couldn't answer. Pearl's going to be a convert, she pretended she really wanted to know about theology. She said to Sister Matthew: if Mary was the mother of Jesus, and Jesus was the son of God the Father, then Mary must have been married to God the Father. We all giggled a lot. Pearl also asked her what was the sin of Sodom. The next lesson, Sister Superior came in. She said that Sister Matthew was very young and we shouldn't be cruel to her. We all despised Sister Matthew for being so stupid and for telling on us. Then she went off to the Poor Clares to be a contemplative. So now it's Ugly Face who takes us for RE and for recreation. She lets some of us walk up and down with her, and she tells us stories about famous Catholic places like Fatima and Lourdes.

I *wish* I could have a vision of Our Lady. But it's never the people who hope for them who have them. If you passionately want a vision you can be sure you'll never have one. They usually happen to peasant children abroad, gathering wood in the countryside, who haven't a clue it's Our Lady they're seeing until she tells them. I would know straight away.

I am praying and praying to Our Lady that the bell will ring. But it's hopeless. Ugly Face is looking at the clock and remembering that because of what Pope John has said in the Second Vatican Council she has to encourage us to ask lots of questions in RE. So she stops talking and tells us to make comments. Karen and Janice look at each other, then Karen puts her hand up.

It's about Charity, she says, it says in the book that Charity means loving everybody but loving men is wrong Sister isn't it unless you're married and even then you can only love one well Sister is it true what everyone says that Marie's auntie

57

went with men for money she was a whore everyone knows
that it's true isn't it.

4

I always liked the long way home from primary school because
striding along the top of the railway embankment I could
pretend I was a pirate chief sailing over rough seas in search
of booty. That day hunger filled me, the wind in my sails. It
drove me through the long sharp grasses between low coils
of bramble, nettles and dockleaves, the froth of cow parsley.
I skimmed along a narrow path worn by others' feet before
mine. Our route was the same. It led home.

I was in a hurry because I wanted my tea so badly and
because I wanted to ask Auntie to get me some new plimsolls
for Sports Day. Mine were a disgrace, apparently, I had been
told off for looking so scruffy. It was my last term at primary
school, my last Sports Day. I felt I might stand a chance
of winning the hundred yards sprint if I had some new
shoes to run in.

The kitchen was empty. I threw my satchel on the table.
The dog didn't bother barking a welcome, she was too old
and fat, and she was dozing by the grate full of cold ashes. I
called out for Auntie as I ran upstairs, and again as I went
in through her bedroom door.

The room was dim, the curtains drawn against the afternoon
sun. Auntie was resting on the bed. Her eyes were open. A
burning cigarette balanced on the ashtray next to her. She
was wearing her afternoon frock, the one with mauve and blue
flowers on it. It was unbuttoned all down the front. She and the
man with her lay very still, like in a photograph. Perhaps they
were not still, perhaps that is the way I choose to remember

it. I looked at her bare white bosom, at the man who curled in her arms and sucked at one of her breasts like a baby.

I fled back to the embankment, to my hideout in the long grass. When I reappeared later, at the proper time for tea, she slapped me, angrier than I'd ever seen her. Her hand caught me on the cheekbone and left a bruise. We had sardines on toast. Quite soon after that she decided that since I'd won a scholarship to the convent school I might as well be a boarder. That was after the two ladies from the council came to see her. She said I would have to understand it was all for the best. She sat on the stairs and cried. I'd never seen her do that before. It was then that I realised that something was broken, and that I'd done it.

5

I fell in love as fast as possible at university. I chose one of my teachers, because he was a teacher, because he was older, because he was powerful, because he was kindly, because he was glamorous. He took me to Italy. I thought I'd fallen in love with him but it was Italy that captured my heart. I didn't know the difference.

I bought myself a red satin mini-dress with the last of my grant, and gave myself cheekbones with the aid of blusher. Auntie would have called it rouge. She never met my lover because I didn't invite her to. She came up to Cambridge to visit me once and I was ashamed of letting my friends see her. Her old stained mac and her untipped Woodbines and her out-of-date slang. I punished her for all this, and more, by keeping aloof, not bothering to write. By then she'd moved to Manchester, anyway, and we met rarely. I preferred it that way.

I left my lover on that first trip abroad together. We went to Rome, so that he could attend a conference on linguistics and Renaissance poetry. By day he attended seminars and lectures and I went sightseeing. I kept company with saints, virgins, sibyls, hermaphrodites, angels, madonnas. It was the long vacation, Alice had gone to Switzerland with her parents and Mary was in Greece with her boyfriend, I knew no one in Rome. In the evenings we had dinner with my lover's colleagues from the conference. Understanding little of their talk I was mostly silent. I concentrated on the food. At night my lover worked and I read novels.

One day, bored with being a tourist, I accompanied my lover to the Herziana library at the top of the Spanish Steps. Waiting for him to finish work, I flicked through an old book of engravings I picked at random from the shelf. Allegories. The battle of the soul. The Virtues. There she was, Mrs Charity, feeding four babies from her bare white breast and no black square stuck over it. For some reason, that evening I rang Auntie in Manchester from the hotel. I learned that her funeral had been the week before. Lung cancer. She'd never mentioned it.

Next morning, having made my phone call to Mary's mother's niece in Vicenza, I left my lover a note, got on a train and fled north. In the hot steamy weather of mid-August we stuck to the fake-leather seats. The carriage was packed with young men on military service going home on leave, talking and laughing, sharing bottles of beer. Sweat rolled down my armpits and my forehead, disguised my tears. Outside the scratched window the tightly strung vines were pale with heat, the hills a blue blur.

Opposite me, wedged in between the soldiers, sat a plump countrywoman and her plump daughter. The latter wiped away great drops of perspiration from her face, wriggled and sighed. I could see that she felt her clothes were too many and too tight. Finally she leaned aside and whispered in her mother's ear. The mother nodded, and busied her hands at her daughter's back, lifting, searching. The daughter blushed and held her head high. She moved one big shoulder, then the other, then shook herself. Triumphantly the mother slid the daughter's bra from out of the back of her clothes. The daughter laughed in relief and pleasure. The soldiers had noticed nothing. I saw Auntie's impassive face as she lay on the bed holding her man-baby. Behind my copy of *Middlemarch* I was still crying but I was laughing too. The daughter slept, head on her mother's arm.

Once we were beyond Florence and had emerged from the tunnels cut through the mountains, the weather broke. Freak thunderstorms tumbled into each other high above our heads. At Bologna the station was flooded, the underpass blocked. People waded ankle deep across the railway lines to clamber on to their trains. We reached Vicenza in the early evening. Gabriella met me at the station. She seemed quite unsurprised by my phone call, without fuss invited me to stay until I decided what to do next.

We walked through the warm rainy streets under her umbrella. Once in the centre of the city we went along under the colonnades over gleaming grey paving stones. She took me into the Caffè Garibaldi, bought me black coffee and a brandy, sat next to me at the little round marble-topped table while I finished crying. All around us smartly dressed women lit cigarettes and gossiped. Gabriella's head was close to mine. I looked at her big rosy mouth, her flopping dark hair, her square amber earrings, and gulped down my brandy. She began to smile. She nodded at me, waited for me to speak.

Blurting out my story in faulty childish Italian, I discovered that I could make myself understood. I was alone and separate now, no kindly academic lover to translate for me, mediate between me and the world. Talking in Italian felt truer than my usual English speech. Because another woman sat there, delicate and solid, and listened to me with interest and wanted me to go on. Opening my mouth, I tasted ash, I bit into shards of glass, I swallowed dust. The word Auntie meant a warm flannelette back in bed, a tobacco kiss, yet the bed was empty and her mouth gone. I stumbled along, finding Italian words one after the other, rolling them, sour milk, over my tongue: Mrs Charity has had to turn her back, Mrs Charity has had to shut her bedroom door, Mrs Charity has had to go away. I grabbed one of Gabriella's cigarettes and sucked on it.

We crossed the Piazza dei Signori in the steamy drizzle, arm in arm under the umbrella again, Gabriella talking to me about her childhood in the south. Her small flat, high up in a shabby palazzo just round the corner, had a chipped marble floor and was walled with books. She showed me the shower, the bed, and left me, propping the door open. A shaft of golden light slid in. Wrapped in a quilt, fenced round with pillows, I dozed in the half-dark, listening to the mutter of her typewriter, the soft gaiety of *Don Giovanni* on the record-player. Soon, she'd told me, she'd come in to wake me. We'd have a glass of wine, think about dinner. Her friend Filippo was coming to take us to a restaurant. Until then, rest. The darkness held me like a pair of warm strong arms.

Our Lady of Perpetual Succour Mrs Charity Auntie my young erotic mother.

FISH

There was a giant on the causeway. I watched him stride into the sky, the plumy reeds of the marsh rippling away from his right boot, and the sea, boiling up the colour of old tea, splashing back from his left. The causeway trembled as he pounded along it and the gulls wheeled off over his bristling black hair.

Once he had dwindled to human size I let go of my breath, clapped shut the back door, and returned to the queer kitchen that curved like a crescent moon. Only standing at the stove could you see both the sink and the china cupboard. Standing at one end you lost the other. The wall in the middle bulged out and hid it.

My mother fetched an egg from the black wire basket that

hung in the larder, cracked it on the edge of a cup, made the yolk slip from one half of the shell to the other, let the white dangle down, plop.

Her lips changed from thin and compressed to relaxed, plump. When she moved her head a little I thought she was still trying out the effect of air moving over her bare nape. All the way back from Ipswich on the bus yesterday she had undulated her neck like a swan, one hand constantly going up to ruffle the newly short crop to search for the non-existent chignon. She'd let me finger it too, soft as swan's feathers. Now to her beauty she had added a dash of the boy, silky spikes sticking up where she'd rumpled them tracing the memory of hairpins. There were fine wrinkles about her mouth, prominent when she was cross but smoothing themselves out, as now, when she unclenched her jaw and began to smile again. The skin under her deep-set eyes was puckered, a little parched. When she remembered to she slapped beeswax on to the furniture, saddle-soap on to her boots, cream on to her face. Her cheekbones were smooth as eggs. In the summer she went brown on the first day of hot sunshine.

Today, sun and rain sparkled on the windowpane together. She was making a sauce to go with the fish and broccoli we were going to have for lunch, even though we'd only just finished breakfast. She was breathing deeply, still not quite calmed down. Sauces thickened with egg yolk, she'd explained to me many times, curdled easily, if the cook was in too much of a hurry, or cross, or overheated the mixture. I watched, to see what would happen. I perched next to her, my head close to her, so that I could brush my cheek against the coarse thick cotton of her apron, snuff up her smell that was a mixture of sweat, eau-de-Cologne and warm animal.

She tilted the bowl in which the egg yolk sat, propped it

on the edge of the breadboard, held the bowl steady with one hand, and whisked with the other. I held ready the little pan of melted butter, and, when she grunted, began to tip it in, drop by drop, while she beat it with her fork.

– There now, she coaxed: you're coming along really nicely, that's it, gently does it, lovely.

The egg yolk and the butter responded. She called it performing. They flowed together and thickened, and she praised them again.

– Quick, she said to me: now fetch the pan of fish stock and we'll drip in some of that.

I hesitated. She dropped the fork on the tabletop.

– Bloody hell. We haven't got any bloody fish because your bloody father was supposed to go and get it before breakfast and he bloody well forgot.

The egg yolk and the butter, bereft of her attention, began to separate. Smoothness and lightness broke up into little oily grains in a sort of yawn, a yellow ripple of defiance.

– That's that, my mother said.

She untied the strings of her apron and threw it over the back of the kitchen chair.

– Why the hell am I thinking about lunch anyway? I must be daft.

She put out a finger and stroked the side of my neck, ear to shoulder.

– I'm no good for anything in a state like this. I'll be better off doing some writing, not faffing about down here.

She hugged me. I bit her forearm quite hard, holding the fold of skin between my teeth the way our neighbour's dog held his newspaper, pretending to worry it. She tasted of bed. She hadn't had a bath this morning. They'd overslept. That was one of the reasons my father had been

65

so cross. Another was her having her hair cut off without asking him first.

At the first turn of the stairs she paused, to yell down to me.

– If you want to play outside don't go too far away. Stay close to the house, OK?

I pretended not to hear. She tramped on up.

Our house was right at the end of the promenade, where the pink-washed cottages stopped and the sea wall began. It used to be the coastguards' lookout. It was like a lighthouse in shape, a stumpy tower with a little rounded cap like a mushroom's. Inside it the staircase coiled round and up. On the ground floor were our curved kitchen and sitting-room, and the lean-to shed built on the side that my father used as a studio. Above this was the lodger's bedroom and the bathroom, and above that, piled on top of each other, were my parents' bedroom, my bedroom, and my mother's study. At the moment, because it was the start of winter, we had no lodgers and so we were broke. That was another reason my parents had had the row last night. Shouting above the noise of the radio so that I could easily hear them next door in the kitchen where I was pretending to do some drawing.

My mother's study was the best room in the house, snug and round, with portholes, and a little white metal balcony. You had to climb up a ladder to get to it. She insisted on having it when we moved in because being right at the top of the house it was far away from my father and me. My father could paint with us listening to the radio on the other side of the open door, but my mother said she could only write when she felt completely alone. We weren't allowed in her study without her. She said we'd only mess it up. She had lovely things on her desk: little china pots, glass paperweights, a box of old nibs, a wineglass full of felt-tip pens, a red straw basket full of notebooks. It was where she went to get away from us, not only to write children's books. Sometimes on Sundays when she went up to dust I'd go with her, and she'd show me her things one by one and let me play with them.

I stood in the hall, wondering what to do. Then I saw she'd left her purse on the hall table. I decided to give her a surprise and go to fetch the fish.

I liked her purse. Worn leather sides fastened together at the top with a gilt clasp like two hands that you could click and unclick in the palm of your hand. Inside was a concertina of compartments of thin pink leather, soft as the chamois she used for cleaning the windows. Coins in one part, notes in the next, bus tickets, cinema tickets, library tickets, an old drawing of mine folded up small with dirty creases. It was a picture of her I'd done at infant school. I smoothed it out to look at it, as I always did when she gave me my pocket money. I was a good drawer, everyone said so. In the picture she had long hair, almost down to her waist. It wasn't right any more, so I tore it up and threw the pieces on the floor.

My socks were too short. The wellingtons were cold against my legs when I shoved my feet into them. I couldn't find Jeremy's lead, so I tied a piece of string on to his collar instead.

Ten steps, and I was on the beach. The sky was full of big black clouds dashing across the sun, and it was very windy. The tide was running out. I hauled Jeremy down over the shingle and on to the wet sand which was easier to walk on. There were no other dogs around so I let him off his piece of string. So far I hadn't managed to stop him wanting to fight with other dogs. He was invisible to everyone but me but other dogs always knew he was there and went for him. My father kicked them if they came too close. I wished I'd brought his stick out with me. I was thinking of the fierce Alsatian that sometimes appeared. Then I remembered the red mark my teeth had made on my mother's arm and started to whistle. I was practising in secret to surprise my father who said I was hopeless at it, girls of eight couldn't whistle and never to let him hear that screeching again.

I turned my back on our house and the causeway and the marsh beyond it and walked along close to the sea. I knew I wouldn't get lost. I would walk along as far as the fishing boats and then come back. There was no reason to hurry. On Saturday mornings the fishermen sold their catch right up until lunchtime, and it was still early. I splashed through the waves for a bit, until I got water down my boots, and then I went higher up the beach to the tideline. There was a good lot of driftwood today. I collected as much as I thought I'd be able to drag home, tied it together with my piece of string, and left it for my return journey. I was already cold, because I'd forgotten to put my windcheater on, but I was determined to stay out as long as possible. Until my mother missed me and started shouting for me, thinking I was lost.

I started to look for shells and the green bits of broken bottle, rubbed smooth by the sea, that I called jewels. I found a lot of pebbles covered with sticky black tar, a couple of dry cuttlefish, a dead seagull, several rotting fish-heads. I found just one good stone, a lump of pink quartz still glistening with sea water.

Because I was keeping my eyes down I almost bumped into the cable. It stretched across my passage, barring it. A tight twist of thick steel, two feet off the slope of the beach. One end ran straight into the sea, a little way out, and disappeared in the yellow-grey waves, and the other went tautly over the top of the hill of shingle and vanished.

My legs were tired. I sat down, propped myself against the slide of damp stones, and put my hands lightly about the cable.

It was alive. Inside the tunnel of my clasp it throbbed and vibrated. It was a cord that shook with messages in sea language. I was connected to it. I had tied myself on to the end of it, and now I belonged to the sea. I was cast up on the beach, but the sea could easily pull me back into itself if I just let go, let myself go with the tide. I would float in the wild water, I would be carried close to the sea's heart.

But perhaps it was I who held the cable and did the pulling. Perhaps it was I who would lean back and haul like the fishermen did when they winched up their boats. What had I caught? A sloppy pale blob like a jellyfish, with long tentacles that stung, and an enormous open mouth like a shark's, razor-teeth ready to bite me, to eat me up. As bad as the Alsatian dog who might appear at any moment.

I sat very still in case anything was looking at me. Like in my dream last night. When I watched. It woke me up, and I found I'd wet the bed. It just washed through me, I couldn't stop it, rushing and warm, then I woke up cold and stinking. I was so ashamed I started crying. My mother heard me and came down. She found me some clean pyjamas and changed my sheets and put me back to bed. She promised to stay with me until I went back to sleep again. She said I couldn't sleep in her bed.

It had started to drizzle. There was wet trickling down the back of my neck now as well as in the bottom of my boots. I jumped to my feet and shouted for Jeremy.

At the fish stall at the top of the beach I looked at the lobsters, still alive, waving their claws, and chose cod, because

69

it was well dead. The fisherman wrapped it up for me in a sheet of newspaper, a damp parcel smelling of the sea. I tucked it under my arm and went to collect my bundle of driftwood.

The front door, unlatched, swung open easily, like the door of my parents' room in my dream last night. My father must have walked off his bad temper and come home. I put the fish on the larder shelf, dumped the wood next to the boiler where Jeremy was already settled in his basket, and went to look for my parents in the studio.

They weren't there, though the oil heater was on. My father had been tidying up. He'd washed all his brushes and pots and laid them out neatly on the big shelf under the window. There was still dust everywhere, and paint splashes thick on the lino, and bits of wood, paper and canvas littering the corners. I knew what he meant when he said he liked working in a bit of a mess. It made him feel comfortable.

Now he was teasing my mother about housework. I could hear his voice booming through the sitting-room door. I stood in the doorway and watched them.

My giant father was lying on the sofa in front of the fireplace reading the newspaper. He was so long, lying down, that his feet hung over the end. My mother was scuttling about impatiently emptying ashtrays, throwing dead flowers into the fire, plumping up cushions. Her hair stood up in spikes as though she'd been running her fingers through it. I saw my father eyeing it.

– What's for lunch? he was roaring: I'm starving, woman. Do I have to do everything myself?

He was laughing and now so was she. She shook the crumbs off the hearthrug into the fire. In just the time

I'd been standing at the door she'd made the place look welcoming again. She turned towards him and saw me. She advanced on me and picked me up in her strong arms, and I swung, loose and collapsed as a jellyfish, between her hands.

YOUR SHOES

I thought I knew you as well as I know this house. No secret
places, no hidey-holes, nothing in you I couldn't see. Now
I realise how you kept yourself from me, how I didn't really
know you at all.

You're not here any longer so how can I speak to you? You
can't speak to someone who isn't there. Only mad people talk
to an empty chest of drawers, a bed that hasn't been slept in
for weeks. Someone half-mad, with grief that is, might pick up
a shoe from the rug and hold it like a baby. Someone like me
might do that. As if the shoe might still be warm or give a clue
to where you've gone. One shoe pointed in fact towards the
bedroom window, the view of the front garden, and the other

pointed towards the door. They wanted to get out, to get away, just like you did. I made them neat again, I stowed them in the wardrobe. Just in case. I locked the wardrobe door on those rebellious shoes. They could be like me and grieve in the darkness. For a bit. Then I let them out. I'm not cruel. But they've got to learn, haven't they. Kids these days. Well.

I can't send you a letter, either, because I don't know your address. There's no point really in writing this because it can't reach you. You have to live in a house with a front door and a letter-box if the postman is to deliver mail, and I don't suppose you do. It's not very likely, is it, you've found yourself a place. I don't know where you are. You just went off, just ran out of the house in the middle of the night, and left me.

It costs me a lot to admit that, can't you understand? If I wrap my arms around myself and hold tight it keeps the pain in. Stops it spilling out and making a terrible mess. If I keep my mouth pursed tight I can't scream or throw up. If I imagine that you're gone for good, that you'll never come back, then this terrible wailing sound will begin and never stop, I might go mad. At least this paper has ruled lines my writing can't fall off.

If you opened the door now and came in you'd find me here in your room. I'm lying curled up in the middle of the bed, on top of the duvet. I've drawn the curtains because the light hurts my eyes. It's already lunchtime but I don't want to face the fridge, the freezer, the microwave. I'm not hungry. I'm better off here, looking at the locked wardrobe door. Your shoes are standing outside it now, side by side. The right shoe on the right-hand side and the left shoe on the left. In their proper places, no fuss, like a husband and wife. I'd like you to get married one day, I'd like you to have a normal life, of course I would. I've tied the shoes' laces together so they won't get separated or lost. White laces, that I washed and ironed.

What did you have for lunch today? I hope you ate something. Did you beg for the money to buy a burger or a sandwich? I'd like to think you had a proper lunch. Something hot. Soup, perhaps, in a Styrofoam cup. You used to love tinned tomato soup. Cream of. I always urged you to eat proper meals, meat and two veg or something salady, when you got home from school. You liked snacks better as you got older, it was the fashion amongst your friends I think, all day long you ate crisps and buns and I don't know what, at teatime when you came in you'd say you weren't hungry then late at night I'd catch you raiding the kitchen cupboards. Fistfuls of currants and sultanas you'd jam into your mouth, one custard cream after another, you'd wolf all my supply of chocolate bars.

How do you feed yourself out there on the street? You're too young to get a job, who'd have you and what could you possibly do? What do you have to do to be fed? Do you have to go with men, is that it? How else could you get the money if you don't beg? There are so many of you begging for the money to buy food, stands to reason there isn't enough to go round. People don't like being continually asked, do they, they don't like being treated like bottomless pits. These days you have to choose who to give money to. I don't mean the starving millions in Africa, I mean the people of your age hanging about outside the supermarkets and the tube stations up in London, around the railway stations, I've seen the photos

75

in the newspapers, it's not very nice having to imagine you mixing with people like that. Drug addicts and so on. You're fifteen years old. What do those men make you do? What do you have to do to get money for food?

Your father didn't mean it when he told you those things the other night. You've got to understand, he lost his temper and used some unfortunate expressions. At your age I'm sure I wouldn't have known the meaning of any of those words. As a young girl I'd have been hit if I used such language as I've heard you use. I was very old-fashioned. Square, they called it then. I grew up in a very old-fashioned family. Of course we had marvellous times together but my father was very strict. It didn't do me any harm. There was no truancy in our family in those days I can assure you, we simply wouldn't have dared. It was unthinkable. Not like you and your friends. We weren't spoilt. Not like your generation. These enormous presents at Christmas and so on. There wasn't the money. Your father works himself nearly to death for his family, for us. Because he loves us and wants us to have what he didn't. Little luxuries. What you and your lot take for granted. And me with my teaching job, I've done my bit for you too. We've given you everything a child could possibly want.

I'm sure you'd never have left if you realised I'd be this upset. You didn't mean to hurt me, did you. You never meant to make me so unhappy I'm sure. It was that mob you got in with at school. That Vanessa for instance. I wouldn't be surprised to hear she's on drugs. She had that look. You're so innocent, you didn't realise. You're too trusting, too kind, you don't know what these people can be like.

*

76

People pretend to be kind but they're ghouls. They ring up to see how I am and I can hear them gloat. It's not their fifteen-year-old daughter who's left home and gone off God knows where. The doctor's given me something to help me sleep and I've taken a week's sick leave from school. I try to put on a cheerful face. Oh, I say: she'll be back soon, I'm sure of it, why, she hasn't even taken her new shoes!

I don't think you have a clue how we feel. Just because we're not ones for letting it all out in public doesn't mean we don't live with this terrible pain. We don't speak of it much. But of course we know how each other feels. We have to be brave, we have to get on with living. The doctor told me: try to live from day to day. That's what they tell dying people too, I've heard it on a radio programme on hospices. You're not to die, d'you hear. You're alive somewhere aren't you. Sooner or later you'll ring up won't you from wherever you are. Some squat full of dropouts and drug addicts. Some cardboard box under a bridge. Some pile of filth. Of course they wouldn't have telephones there, I know that, you know what I mean. My daughter sleeping on a pile of filth I can't bear it.

You've got to understand. When your father called you a dirty slut he didn't mean you to take it personally. It was just a manner of speaking. In the heat of the moment. He adores you, you know that. It's just that he feels protective of you, and he can't stand being answered back. He can't stand rudeness. Not from you, not from anybody. What did you expect, being brought home drunk at three in the morning? We were half out of our minds with worry, of course we were upset. I've always thought of you as just an empty-headed blonde, I've never thought you were really bad. Then I find out that you

77

drink alcohol at parties and smoke pot. Of course your father was angry. After all this is his house. You shouldn't have got so upset. I'm sure he didn't mean all of what he said.

I dreamed of my mother last night. There was so much I wanted to say to her and now it's too late. Daughters ought to be close to their mothers. I wasn't to mine. She was a very stupid woman. She never had much of an education, then the war came and she joined up. I've still got a photo of her in uniform. Blonde hair done up in sausages on top of her head, cap stuck on one side, big lipsticked mouth. A plump woman with a loud jolly laugh. Fat, let's be honest. Terribly vulgar, always saying the wrong thing then laughing. My poor father used to wince. He shouldn't have married her, he should have chosen someone more like himself. Then I might have had a better childhood.

My mother was like you, she liked a drink. She used to do the housework with a cigarette hanging out of her mouth, then she'd put her feet up and have a gin and tonic. She was very clean, I'll give her that, she kept us and the house spotless. She never had much time for me, I was just a girl, she preferred my brother. She thought I should be a housewife like her but I surprised everybody by getting into college to do domestic science. She brought me up to know how to fill bridge rolls for parties, how to make Yorkshire pudding for Sunday lunch. Then I went ahead of her and learned about nutritional science. Miss La-di-Da she used to call me. I was thin, rather plain. I was fair like her, but my hair was straight. She had hers dyed more and more golden. She had a bouffant perm. The face powder used to collect in the creases of her cheeks and melt. Then she'd powder over it. She wore a girdle to hold herself in. She lived her whole married life in a suburb in a detached house with four bedrooms and she thought it was heaven. Well, she would, after the semi-slum she grew up in up north. She was jealous because I loved my father more than her. We'd go for walks in the park together. We talked about things she couldn't understand.

It always hurt me, how nice she was to you. She spoiled you. She loved you more than she loved me. It isn't fair. That was the cry of my girlhood. I had to help with the housework but my brother did nothing. I was always racing to get done so I could go out with my father. He took me to the golf club and introduced me to all his friends. Once he took me to the pub. He told me I was bright and had a real future ahead of me. I swore that when I grew up I wouldn't be like my mother. Well at least I've kept my figure. I'm not fat like she was. She wore the most unsuitable clothes. Always whatever was in fashion, regardless, she liked bright colours, lots of costume jewellery, she looked a bit of a tart, let's face it, stiletto heels, charm bracelets, the lot.

You've got small feet just like mine. Like hers. All the women in our family have small feet. Sturdy, with a strong arch and short toes. For a couple of years now I've been able to buy your shoes without having to drag you round the shops. Moan whine, after ten minutes in Marks you'd threaten you were going to faint and I had to get you out into the fresh air. They're lovely, these shoes I bought you. White trainers, you see I know what you like. I thought you'd love them. I'm looking after them for you. I've got them under the duvet with me now. I'm keeping an eye on them, oh yes. They are perfect because they're new, they've never been worn.

*

I had a white wedding. My father had been saving for it for years, he said nothing was too good for his little girl. He gave me away, I walked down the aisle on his arm feeling numb. I married your father on the rebound, everybody knew that. I was desperately in love with Pete, he was the great love of my life, when he went off and left me I thought I might as well marry your father. He was always there in the background, he'd been waiting for me. He's been a good husband, a good father. Everyone said how lucky I was. Of course I never told my mother I wasn't a virgin, she'd have had fifty fits. My father would have killed me if he'd known.

Of course I wanted you. Of course I love you. It's hurtful and wicked to say I don't. I suppose it's my fault you've left home to sleep rough God knows where. Go on, blame your mother, everyone else does. I'm a failure as a mother. I didn't give you enough of whatever it was. You've always been very difficult. I did my best, what more could I do? Next thing you'll be saying it's because I didn't breastfeed you, or because I didn't pick you up every time you cried. You can't imagine what it was like. At night you cried so much, in the end I used to shut the door on you and go back downstairs. I was exhausted. Your father slept through most of it, he said it wasn't his job. Just like my father. He wasn't interested in me when I was little, then when I was older and showed I had a brain, that was when he got involved. Oh but we did have a lot of happy times too, I know we did. Don't forget that. I wish you wouldn't sulk. I wish you'd stop sulking and answer me.

It's cosy in here. Peaceful, too. I've unplugged the telephone so that I can concentrate on you and we shan't be disturbed.

80

It'll be dark soon, the street lamps have just come on, I can see one shining through the curtains. Funny, you never did like these curtains. I remember I got them in a sale up in town, I thought they were lovely, really modern with these splashes of blue and grey, they were exactly what I'd have wanted as a girl. Then when you came home and saw what I'd done you flew into a temper, you said you wanted the old curtains back. By then it was too late, I'd thrown them away. I'd gone to so much trouble to give you a surprise, I couldn't believe you'd be so ungrateful. Then you had to go and burst into floods of tears, that was the last straw, oh you used to be so unkind to me. Throwing my presents back in my face.

At first I kept the shoes in the box I made them pack them in at the shop, tenderly wrapped in tissue-paper. Delicate white sheets, rustling, uncreased. Then I tried them in the wardrobe, then side by side on the rug. They're best in here with me I think, safe and warm in bed. Tucked up tight.

How could you do that to us. How could you. Boasting about it even. I think you wanted us to find out. Thank God I had the sense to look in your bag that night. You laughed at me, you said lots of girls in your class had had sex by the time they were fifteen, you weren't going to be the exception.

After my mother died I had to clear out her clothes and pack them up for jumble. Her shoes hurt me so much. Rows of high-heels, all of them too small for her, she was so vain, all of them moulded to the shape of her poor feet. You could see how her toes were all bent over, misshapen. Bulges where she'd had bunions, corn-plasters. Who'd have wanted them? I threw them all in the dustbin. Then on the way home I stopped

81

the car and bought you a pair of new shoes as a surprise, really beautiful ones, the best I could afford.

Your father will be home soon. I've locked the bedroom door so that he can't get in. I want to be alone with you for a bit. My darling girl whom I love so much. I hold you to my breast and rock you like my mother never rocked me. You're so small and pale. Let me hold you while you cry.

Laces like strings of white liquorice. They taste sweet.

There, my darling, there. You're at home with mother, everything's all right. I knew you'd come back, I knew you'd come back to me.

I love you I love you so much oh yes oh yes.

THE BISHOP'S LUNCH

The angel of the resurrection has very long wings. Their tips end in single quills. The angel of the resurrection has three pairs of wings that swaddle him in black shawls then unwrap when he needs them, nervous and strong. The angel of the resurrection flies in the darkness. He is invisible and black. His feathers are soft as black fur.

That is what Sister Josephine of the Holy Face was thinking early on that Wednesday morning of Holy Week four days before Easter. Uncertain whether or not her picture of the angel was theologically sound, she decided that she would record it later on in her little black notebook, the place where she was required to write down all her faults. These were confessed at a weekly interview with the Novice Mistress and were then atoned for by suitable penances. The little black notebook was one of the few items Sister Josephine had been allowed to bring with her from home when she entered the convent seven months previously. Her mother had put it in her suitcase herself, along with a new missal and four pairs of black woollen stockings.

A thought which Sister Josephine of the Holy Face knew she would not write down in the little book was that she ought to be called Sister Josephine of the Unholy Stomach. At home on the farm eight kilometres inland from Etretat she had drunk her breakfast *café au lait* from a china bowl stencilled with blue flowers. She had eaten warm crusty bread fetched half an hour before from the village bakery. On Sundays there was hot chocolate after High Mass, with brioche or galette, and a hearty appetite seen as a good thing. Here in the convent on the outskirts of Rouen the day-old bread was always stale, and the thin coffee bitter with chicory and drunk from a tin cup.

Angels, having no bodies, were not tormented by memories of *saucisson* and cold fresh butter, of thick sourish cream poured over cod and potatoes, over beans, over artichokes. Yet the black feathers of the wings of the angel of the resurrection were very soft.

Sister Josephine was down on her hands and knees in front of the cupboard under the big stone sink of the convent kitchen, groping inside it for the bread-knife she had unaccountably mislaid. Her fingers closed over a bunch of silky plumage. It wasn't an angel's wing, she discovered when she brought it out, but the feather duster she had lost a month ago. Her penance for that had been to kiss the ground in the refectory before breakfast every day for a week. The taste of floor polish. She shivered as she remembered it.

The bell rang for chapel. Sister Josephine spotted the bread-knife hiding behind a bucket of washing soda. Squatting back on her haunches, she flung it, with the feather duster, on to the wooden table behind her. Then she straightened up, untied the strings of her heavy blue cotton apron, and hung it on the nail behind the door. Not *my* apron, she reminded herself: *ours*.

She glided along the dark cloister as rapidly as she dared. She wasn't supposed to begin her kitchen duties so early, but she'd wanted to get on with slicing up the long baguettes into the bread-baskets ready for breakfast. There was too much work in the kitchen for one person to do, even in such a small community, but to complain would be a sin against obedience. Putting Sister Josephine in sole charge of the cooking, the Novice Mistress had announced six weeks earlier, was a real test of her faith. And of the nuns' digestions, Sister Josephine had muttered to herself.

She knelt in her stall, amongst the other novices, yawning as she tried to follow the still unfamiliar Latin psalms. Her empty stomach growled, and she clasped her hands more tightly together. They were chilblained, and smelt of carbolic soap. Now they looked like her mother's hands: red, roughened by work. Her mother's hands were capable, quick and deft for the labour of farmyard and house. They were expert at cooking, too. She was famous among the village women for the lightness of her choux pastry, the *gougères* and eclairs she turned out on feast-days. Sister Josephine had resisted all her mother's attempts to teach her the domestic arts. She had refused to believe that God wanted her to serve Him through topping and tailing beans, peeling potatoes. She'd hungered for transcendence, for the ecstasy of mystical union. She hadn't come to the convent to *cook*.

What in heaven, Sister Josephine asked herself for perhaps

the hundredth time that Lent, am I going to do about the Bishop's lunch?

It was an ancient tradition in the convent that every year on Easter Sunday the Bishop of the diocese would say High Mass in the convent chapel and then join Reverend Mother, the Novice Mistress and the other senior nuns at their table in the refectory for the midday meal. To celebrate the end of the rigorous fasting of Lent and the presence of such a distinguished guest, and, of course, the resurrection of the Saviour from the dead, an elegant array of dishes was always served. Sister Josephine knew that the Bishop, like all holy men of the cloth, had renounced the pleasures of the flesh, but she knew too that nonetheless he would expect to be given exquisite food just so that he could demonstrate his indifference to it as he ate.

Help me, she prayed: please help me.

Normally she did not bother God with problems over lost feather dusters and bread-knives and how to turn a few cabbages and turnips into a nourishing soup for twenty hungry nuns. God, being male, was above such trivia. But the Bishop's lunch was an emergency. It was better to bypass Our Lady and the saints this time, to go straight to the top.

The smell of incense, pungent and sweet, made her open her eyes. Morning Mass had begun and she hadn't even noticed. Daydreaming again. Another fault to note down in her little black book. Sighing, she reached into the skirt pocket of her habit, drew it out, and opened it hastily at random. Her stubby black pencil hovered over the page. She drew in a sharp quick breath, and then released it.

Maundy Thursday passed peacefully, apart from the gardener mentioning to Reverend Mother that someone had taken his old and rusty rifle from its usual place in the shed, and that someone else had thoughtfully weeded all the wild sorrel from under the apple trees in the orchard.

On Good Friday the gardener told Reverend Mother he'd heard rifle shots coming from the field backing on to the kitchen garden. Also, the traps he'd laid for rabbits, all three of them, had been sprung by some poacher. And when he went to investigate a great squawking in the chicken shed, he found that the best layers among the hens had been robbed of all their eggs. There would be none to take to market the following week.

Reverend Mother sighed. She was getting old, and tired, and did not want to be faced with all these practical problems. She consoled the gardener as best she could. Then she sent for Sister Josephine. How, she enquired of the young novice, was she going to manage to make a lunch on Easter Sunday fit for a Bishop to eat? Well, Sister Josephine explained: I have been praying for a miracle.

All through that Good Friday afternoon the nuns knelt in the gloomy chapel, all its statues shrouded in purple and its candles extinguished, following the Passion of the Saviour as he was stripped and scourged, crowned with thorns, and then forced to carry his heavy cross up the hill to Calvary. Finally he was nailed to the cross, and hung from it. The nuns sang the great dialogues of the Church, taken from the Old Testament, between Christ and his God, Christ and his people. *My people, what have you done to me? Answer me.* Rain beat at the chapel windows. Christ cried out for the last time and then died. The nuns filed from the chapel, ate their frugal supper, the only meal of the day.

On Holy Saturday Christ was in the tomb and Sister Josephine was in the kitchen. Swathed in her blue apron, she scrubbed the sink, the table, the floor. Then, on the table, she laid out certain items from her *batterie de cuisine*: a wooden spoon, an egg whisk, several long, very sharp knives.

The rabbits she had taken from the gardener's traps were hanging in the pantry. Swiftly she skinned them, one by one, then cut them up and threw them into a pot with a bunch of herbs and half a bottle of communion wine. Next she fetched the pigeons she had shot two days earlier, plucked and trussed them, and arranged them on a bed of apples in a well-buttered dish. Finally she prepared a small mountain of potatoes and leeks, washed a big bunch of sorrel and patted it dry in a cloth, and checked that the two dozen eggs she had removed from the hens were safe in their wicker basket in the store-room.

When the knock came on the back door of the kitchen she was ready. Opening it, she smiled at the boy who stood there, at the silvery aluminium churn and squat bottle he clasped in his arms. The boy's eyes were as blue as hers, his nose as aquiline, his chin as determined. They kissed each other on both cheeks. Sister Josephine took the churn and the bottle, smiled at the boy again, and shut the door on him. Now everything was as ready for tomorrow as it could be.

Very early next morning, just before dawn, the nuns gathered outside the chapel to see the New Fire lit in the cold windy courtyard. Now the great candle, symbol of the risen Christ, could blaze in the darkness. Easter Sunday had arrived. Now the chapel could be filled with flowers and lights, the dark coverings taken off the statues, and the altars hung with lace and white brocade.

The Bishop, with his retinue, arrived to say High Mass. The organ pealed, the nuns stood up very straight in their stalls and sang a loud psalm of praise: Christ is risen, Christ is risen, alleluia.

This miracle of the Resurrection was repeated in the Mass:

through the actions of his chosen one, his priest, Christ offered his body, his blood, to nourish his faithful children. The Bishop's hands moved deftly amongst his holy cutlery. He wiped the chalice, picked up the silver cruets of water and wine, attended to the incense boat. Alleluia, sang the nuns: Christ has leapt from the tomb. Meanwhile, in the kitchen, Sister Josephine's choux pastry leapt in the oven.

The Bishop's lunch, all the nuns later agreed, was a great and unexpected success. The rabbit pâté, scented with juniper, was exquisite. So too was the dish of roasted pigeons with apples and calvados, the sliced potatoes and leeks baked in cream, the poached eggs in sorrel sauce. But, they unanimously declared, the *pièce de résistance* of the entire banquet was the creation which ended it: the figure of an angel sculpted from choux buns stuck together with caramel and then coated with dark bitter-chocolate cream. His arms were held out wide, and his three pairs of black wings extended behind him. A very noble confection, said the nuns: truly, a miracle.

After finishing the washing-up, Sister Josephine went upstairs to her curtained cell in the novices' dormitory. This was forbidden in the daytime, but she didn't care. She sat on her bed and took out her little black book. She opened it, and leafed through the recipes so carefully written out in her mother's handwriting in its centre pages. Perhaps, Sister Josephine thought, my vocation is to leave the convent, train as a chef, and open my own restaurant.

TAKING IT EASY

For breakfast I had exactly what I fancied: two fat croissants with apricot jam, a piece of baguette with butter and Camembert, a bunch of muscat grapes, and several cups of black coffee with sugar. I consumed this feast very slowly while lying in bed. I'd laid the tray with an antique Quimper cup and saucer and plate. I'd put a vase of pink sweet peas on the nearby chest of drawers, clean sheets on the bed. I'd put on my new nightdress, cau-de-nil silk with pencil shoulder-straps. I was celebrating the start of my new life. I was not going to be half-hearted about it. I was going to do it properly.

The Quimper cup had a sturdy little peasant woman, in cap and striped apron and sabots, painted on its side. A charming design in faded orange, dark blue, green. The glaze was cracked, the edge of the cup chipped. I didn't mind. I enjoyed using something that belonged to Angèle's mother and had been in this house for so many years. The round, lidded sugar-pot was painted with a similar design, and the little plate, and the milk jug. The coffee-pot was tall, two-tiered, in speckled blue enamel. It was a hundred years old. I tilted it to get more coffee out, black and fragrant. I lay back against my lace-edged, linen-covered pillows, alternating bites of grapes with swallows of hot coffee.

Inside Angèle's mother's room I felt both safe and free. My lazy eye noted the sea-green walls, the mirror decorated with frills of turquoise glass, the blue and yellow china candlesticks on either side of it. The wooden floor was painted creamy white. Cool and hard when you walked on it in bare feet. Vases of cut flowers, brought back from the market in Cahors, stood about: pink and mauve and lilac sweet peas, white daisies, white stocks. Sounds from outside filtered through the thin white muslin curtain that flapped against the window and half-obscured it: cocks crew, the church bells chimed, a herd of cows walked past softly jangling their bells and grumbling, women's voices called out to each other. Ten o'clock. I yawned and stretched in my deep soft bed.

Back in London I was always at my desk by ten. I'd take my daughter to her primary school round the corner then return home to race through a few domestic tasks: make the beds, wash up, tidy my room sufficiently so that I could bear to sit in it to work. At some point in the day I'd run to the shops to buy food for supper, to collect shoes from the menders or clothes from the dry-cleaners, to pay the newsagent's bill, and so on. At half-past three my daughter's schoolday was over, and our life together began again. Any writing I wanted to do had to happen between ten and three. I was careful never to waste time. Getting up late was impossible. Drinking too much the night before – forget it! Sex – I rationed myself, not wanting my daughter to see too many strange men in my bed in too quick a succession. I concentrated on my work. Five hours a day were all I had. So I rarely bothered with lunch: sometimes I ate a crispbread at the typewriter, scattering crumbs around my desk; sometimes I forked up a bowlful of salad with one hand while making corrections with the other; sometimes I munched an apple while wrestling with semicolons and full stops. I ate as little as possible because I was always trying to lose weight. And if I ate lunch I felt too sleepy afterwards to write. Sleep and food, my twin enemies; I was determined to give in to neither.

I wrote short stories. I earned a meagre but adequate living. Early on in my career I decided that I would have to do a fair bit of hack work to support what I thought of then as my Serious Art. I ended up writing stories for any magazine that would have them, taking any commission I was offered. I devised a series of pseudonyms for the different sorts of stories I wrote. My science-fiction pieces I signed Alexis K. Triffel. For the women's magazine market I was Dorothy Appleday. Harder-edged Gothic romances went out in the name of Virginia Lindisfarne. Melodramas, another much-maligned genre, were back in fashion: I wrote them as Valda Prykke. Soft porn, both gay and straight, I sold as from the pen of Jay C. Dacey. Under my own name I was going to publish, one day, a collection of short stories rivalling those of Colette and Katherine Mansfield and Jean Rhys all put together. One day. The manuscript stayed in my desk drawer, gathering flesh very slowly. In the meantime I honed my skills as a romance writer and fretted about The Commission.

93

This was the Big One. My chance of a real breakthrough. My story, if I could get it done on time, 'I' in this case being the newly invented Claudia Longmore, would be read out on radio *at peak listening time* as part of a special series featuring really well known writers. This could be the start of Claudia's career in radio! The deadline was two months away. Of course, I said over the telephone: no problem, you're talking to a professional here. I'd been bold enough to ring up and offer a story. Now all I had to do was write it.

There was a problem. For the first time in my hardworking and prolific career I got writer's block. I didn't notice at first. I was busy rereading Guy de Maupassant and trying out the recipes in a new diet book I'd seen recommended in a Sunday newspaper. It promised far-reaching changes to my belly and hips. It promised to make them smaller. The diet involved tiny amounts of plain yoghurt and beans. No alcohol. None of the red wine I loved. I persevered. After two months, the book promised, I'd be slim as a string bean.

– What's up with you? my friend Angèle said to me one afternoon outside the school gates as we waited for our daughters who were each other's best friends: you look really terrible. Are you ill or something?

– I do feel rather weak, I admitted: sort of peculiar and faint a lot of the time.

– You aren't pregnant by any chance? she enquired.

I clapped my hands to my head.

– No, but I've just remembered. I should be. In a manner of speaking. I'm supposed to produce a story for radio in two weeks' time. And it's the summer holidays coming up. Whatever shall I do?

My friend Angèle, unlike several of my other women friends, has no desire to be a writer herself and so does not suffer

from envy of me. Nor do I envy her her solidly middle-class
background, so great is my pride in earning my own living.
So we are able to give to each other without anxiety. Now
Angèle immediately arranged to take my daughter off my
hands for two weeks and offered me the use, for that time,
of her mother's house in south-west France.

– She'll be pleased, Angèle explained: she doesn't go there
often enough, and the house needs living in. She doesn't want
to rent it out, she just likes lending it to friends.

For supper that night my daughter insisted on her usual
beefburger and chips. I toyed with a small bowl of cold beans
dressed with yoghurt. My daughter professed herself delighted
at the prospect of two weeks away from my nagging her to eat
healthy food. When she'd gone to bed I dusted my typewriter
and thought of the story I would write. In France everything
would be all right.

But in France everything was not. The house was certainly
old, secluded, and well equipped, the village in the Lot remote,
antique and savage, my few neighbours friendly but not intru-
sive. Every morning that first week I rose early from my bed in
the little guest-room, did my exercises, drank sugar-free black
coffee and consumed plain yoghurt, then plumped myself
down in front of my typewriter. The guest-room looked over
a parched meadow half choked by weeds and scrub. It was
very quiet. There were no distractions. The walls, painted
white, were blank. My brain teemed with words, opening
sentences, promising scenarios, intriguing characters. But I
couldn't write anything.

I stuck at it. I stayed at the typewriter for eight hours
a day, sometimes even nine or ten, just as I'd yearned to
do in London. I thought I owed myself that: to do what
I'd said I so wanted to. Not a single word struggled on to

paper. On the other hand I lost three more kilos and had cheekbones again.

On the seventh evening Angèle rang me up to say that my daughter was fine and how was I getting on?

– I try and try, I confessed: but nothing happens. And the story's due in a week, oh my God, oh my God.

Angèle's voice was smug.

– Well you know what my brother Jim says, the one who's a painter. You have to make the problem part of the subject. Then it'll turn into being part of the solution. So, obviously, what you should do is write a story about writer's block.

– Oh easy, I scoffed: I bet your brother Jim has never felt this awful inertia, this terrible laziness. I just don't *want* to write this bloody story.

– What would you like to be doing instead? Angèle asked.

My answer burst out.

– I'd like to stay in bed all day, every day, for a week, doing nothing at all. And I'd like to be able to eat as much as I want without getting fat. Or without caring about it. And then, oh yes, I wouldn't mind a bit of cheery sex.

That night I couldn't sleep. The words from my unwritten stories danced mockingly in the corners of the little guest-room where I tossed to and fro on the hard single bed. Hunger jabbed my stomach. I felt my jutting hip-bones and made a decision. And then the next day I caught the bus into Cahors and bought a lot of food, an eau-de-nil silk nightdress, and an armful of cut flowers. That night I slept in Angèle's mother's room.

After my lengthy and delicious breakfast the following morning, I dozed a little, then woke at noon. I had a shower, put my nightdress back on, then pottered downstairs to prepare lunch. Mostly a question of opening little waxed paper packages from the *charcuterie* in Cahors. Back upstairs in my hostess's big comfortable bed, I leaned against the hill of lace-edged pillows and devoured mushroom vol-au-vents, green olives with garlic and herbs, a slab of cold rabbit pâté, and a little dish of *salade composée* masked with glossy golden mayonnaise. I drank wine; I bit into green and purple figs, into redcurrants and cherries. I pulled the shutters close, to block the heat and glare of the sun, then slept for a couple of hours. Sleep so deep, in that sea-green room, that I swam in and out of several long lazy dreams before coasting back to wakefulness. The rest of that afternoon, my windows once again open to the sun, I spent gazing at the room in which I lay, and at the view, framed by the drifting curtain and the window, of blue sky and lime trees. I stayed in bed. I said nothing and spoke to no one.

At six o'clock I got up, had another shower, discarded the silk nightdress in favour of a cotton robe, and poured myself a Kir. I drank it at the window while watching the light change over the village rooftops, the approach of sunset. Then I organised dinner. *Saucisses de Toulouse* with potatoes fried with rosemary and garlic, slices of aubergine dusted with flour then fried in olive oil and served with a spoonful of fresh tomato sauce, a feathery green salad, a pyramid of peaches arranged on reddened vine leaves. Another bottle of the local 'black' wine.

I lived like this for the next three days. I lolled on the big cool bed in my hostess's room, daydreaming, feasting, dozing, staring idly out of the window. I rubbed my face against the plaster of the wall. I painted my toenails coral pink.

One lunchtime, just as I was loading a tray with onion tart, courgette fritters and tomato salad, there was a knock on the front door.

He had blue eyes the same colour as the workmen's clothes he wore, which were splashed with paint.

– I'm Jim, he explained: Angèle's brother. Didn't she tell you I'd be turning up this week? I know you're here to write. I won't disturb you.

Over lunch he enquired about my story.

– I've decided it should be an erotic one, I told him: you know, that's popular just now, women's erotic writing.

– What's the difference between erotic and pornographic? he asked.

I watched him throw nectarines and wine into his mouth.

– Actually it's all highly subjective, I explained: come upstairs if you like and I'll show you.

My story lay scattered across his mother's double bed. White sheets of paper criss-crossed with black writing. Pages thin and crisp as onion skins. They rustled under us as we lay in each other's arms.

– I don't know how the story ends, I said: but I know how it begins.

GOD'S HOUSE

Inside the priest's house it was very dark. I flattened my palms against the invisible air then advanced step by tiptoeing step. I smelt dust and the dregs of wine. I'd left the heat outside. The curved edge of a stone doorway was cold, grazed my cheek. Groping forwards, I encountered glass, a metal catch. With a rattle and squeak of iron bars I undid the shutters, pushed them open. Light drowned me. I saw that I was in a kitchen, bare except for a cooker and oilcloth-covered table. Sunlight fell across glistening brown paint on to my hands. I turned around and leaned back against the windowsill.

I was a burglar. My first break and entry. I wasn't sure what I wanted to steal.

*

I was back with you, in our old house where I'd been born twelve years before. Now a veranda had been added on at the front, bellying forwards into the garden, and your bed had been put there under the dome of glass. Half in and half out. You sat up when you saw me come in, and held out your arms.

– You haven't left yet then, I said.

The room behind us was full of relatives, a sort of party going on. You gestured towards me to come closer. You held all my attention: your lashless monkey eyes that were very bright, your translucent skin, your full, blistered lips, the outline of your head under its fuzz of curls. Everything that there was between us concentrated into that look we exchanged. Above the glass roof was the red sky, the break of dawn.

For a while the road ran through the plain, along the poplar-lined Canal du Midi, and then it rose, as the land lifted itself and became hillier. A straight road, running between golden-green plane trees, towards Spain. The rounded hills, brown and dark yellow, took us up, and up. We swung off the main road on to a smaller one, and one yet smaller.

Our village was called Beauregard-du-Perdu. We turned, as instructed, by the wash-house and fountain, and drove up the main street lined with plane trees. A green tunnel pierced with bits of dancing light. At its top I saw the stone bulk of the church, a rounded doorway decorated with zigzags. To the right, behind low gates of grey metal, was the house my aunt and uncle were renting from some French friends. We recognised it straight away from the photographs. I got out of the car and saw the other house, opposite. No. What I saw was the high wall enclosing it, the steps up to the padlocked wooden door in the wall, worn steps that curved sideways then went up to the church behind. A notice tacked to the door, just above the padlock, said A VENDRE. As I stared, the church bells began to clang out the hour and I started back from their dull, flat noise.

My aunt bent towards me.

– Lily. Would you like to be the one to knock on the neighbour's door and ask for the keys? Show us how well you speak French.

I inspected the gravel under my new shoes that I'd bought for the funeral. The gravel was grey like the metal gates, loose chips under my stiff toes. I lifted a foot and scraped it along the ground.

– No point, my uncle said: here she is anyway.

Our letter of introduction named her as Madame Cabazou, a widow. She came out of the alleyway opposite our house, below the wall with its wooden door and its FOR SALE notice. A blue enamel sign proclaimed that the alley was called Impasse des Saints. Madame Cabazou was as quick as one of the lizards on the hot wall nearby. Small and skinny, eyes black as olives in her brown face, grey hair cut short. Gold daisies in her pierced ears. Her marriage earrings, she told me later on: that she wore every day. Flick flick went her tongue in her mouth as she exclaimed and shook hands and pulled the key from her housecoat pocket and ushered us in. She darted off again with a wave of her hand, a promise to bring us a bowl of plums picked that morning from the trees in her field.

Our holiday home was a little house on three floors, its walls painted a cool blue-grey. Red speckled tiles underfoot downstairs, unpolished wooden floorboards in the two bedrooms. Up here the windows had white shutters that creased up like concertinas and let in long arms of brambles laden with roses, and tiny balconies, no bigger than windowsills, in white-painted wrought iron. The bed in my room was narrow and high, with a white cover. The chairs were old-fashioned, with curvy backs. They broke when you sat on them; they were just for show.

The garden was large considering it was in the middle of a village, my aunt said. It was mainly grass, with flower-beds and tangly shrubs dotted about in it. The solid privet hedge surrounding it was such a dark green it was almost black. Over it reared the plane trees that lined the village street outside. Sage green, almond green, sea green, bottle green, those were the colours of the bushes and plants. The flowers were so bright with the light in them, mauve and pink. The sun dazzling down on the garden at mid-day made it white. Too hot to sit in without a hat. I felt scorched. I preferred the coolness of the broken-down barn with its earth floor, where swallows flashed in and out, quick blue streaks. On the first morning the swallows flew into my room when I was still in bed and I felt welcomed.

I was puzzled when the telephone rang. I hadn't seen one the night before. There it was, by the bed. I lifted the receiver and said hello.

Your voice sounded exactly as it always did.

– Hello, you said back to me: how are you getting on?

– D'you mean to say, I asked: that they've got telephones up there?

You laughed.

– Of course we have. How else could we get in touch? Now come on, I haven't much time, how's your father managing, and how are you?

– Oh he's doing fine, I said: more or less. You know. He's being extra careful when he drives the car.

Why did I say that? I don't know. Just then the church bells began to ring, battering the windowpanes, and your voice faded away under their onslaught.

My aunt and uncle were welded to their white plastic lounging chairs. Turned towards each other, they held hands and chatted. They were pink-faced, melting in the heat. I strolled past them with a wave, went out to explore the village.

The church door seemed locked. I shoved it with my shoulder but its resistance didn't yield. I wandered on past it, paused at an open pair of tall wrought-iron gates, went in.

I was in the cemetery. The village within the village. The houses of the dead neatly arranged side by side. The path ran all the way round, tombs on both sides. Some of the graves were just mounds of earth, with fragile, blackened crosses in crumbling iron at their heads. Others were doors laid down on the ground, thick polished stone bearing pots of pink and red porcelain roses, open porcelain books with gilt letters spelling out the names of the dead. Whole families seemed to be crammed into small tight plots. Some of the graves had photographs in black metal frames. Some had stone angels. One had a crucifix made of tiny black beads.

Madame Cabazou knelt by a shiny slab of white granite. She inserted mauve flowers, like the ones in our garden, into a black vase on top of it. I looked over her shoulder to read her husband's name carved into the stone. Emile.

– He died three months ago, Madame Cabazou said: I'm not used to it yet.

She stood up and clasped my arm. Then she held my hand

in hers. Water shone in her eyes, tipped over, flowed down her cheeks.

Just behind the graves the hills began, high and round, crusted with yellow sunflowers. The landscape crackled with their dark gold and black. The earth was a rich brown. We were high up in a wild and lonely place. From here you could see the Pyrenees, misty blue shapes against the blue sky.

Madame Cabazou wore a black housecoat printed with pink roses. She let go of me and fished a handkerchief out of her pocket. She mopped her eyes.

– The village is dying, she said: we used to have vineyards up there but not any more. Only sunflowers now round here. So all the young ones have gone. Just us old people left. It's good your family has come to stay. You'll liven us up.

– They're not my parents, I told her: they're my uncle and aunt.

Madame Cabazou whistled. An ancient beagle bitch trundled out of the bushes, panting, and followed us down the path. I winced away from her in case she snapped or bit.

– Betty, Betty, good dog, said Madame Cabazou: oh she's a good dog my Betty, all the dogs in the village are good, none of them will harm you, they don't bite.

– My mother's just died, I said in the loudest voice I could manage: so they've brought me away on holiday to be nice to me.

Madame Cabazou stood stock still in the centre of the path and cried some more.

– Oh poor child poor child poor little one.

She hung on to my hand again as she wept. Then she blew her nose and shut the tall gates behind us. The church bells began to clamour out the Angelus. Bash, bash, bash.

– Electronic, said Madame Cabazou: the old lady who used

to ring the Angelus, because her father did before her, she died this spring. No village priest any longer, either. Just one who serves all the villages in turn. The presbytery's been empty for a long time.

She fingered the little silver crucifix slung round her neck on a silver chain and sighed.

– The presbytery? I asked.

– The priest's house, she said: there.

We were going down the stone steps from the side of the church, down into the well of green light under the plane trees. She waved her hand at the high wall beside us, the wooden door let into it. We paused there, on the corner of the alleyway, to say goodbye.

– Oh this heat, she said: I do love it. And it's so good for my arthritis.

She tapped me on the cheek.

– You must have faith. Your mother is with God. We must believe that. She's up there in heaven. She's alive for all eternity.

She hurried off. The old dog lurched along after her, slack-bellied, velvety nose in the dust.

You grasped my hand. We took off together with a swift kick, we whirred into the night sky. Holding on to you I was drawn along, buoyant, an effortless progress under the stars above the wheeling earth.

We flew into the mouth of a dark tunnel. I could see nothing, I gripped your hand, felt cold air stream over my eyelids. You knew your way. You carried us both along, our arms were wings.

– I wanted to show you what dying was like, you said: I wanted you to know. Open your eyes. Look.

Below us, in the tunnel, were hospital beds crowded with sick people. They lay still and silent, faces upturned as we flew past. Then they dwindled behind us, and we burst out of the tunnel back into the soft blackness of the night.

– That was dying, you said: we've gone past death now.

Our curving flight traced the shape of the earth below. We swooped sideways, down. Another opening loomed. Another tunnel? I wasn't sure. The silvery stars rolled past. We were carried on the shoulders of the wind.

– There's a lot more I've got to find out about, you explained: I've got a lot more to explore. Come on, let's go in here next.

A mosquito whined in my ear. I cursed and sat up. You were no longer there.

We ate lunch in the garden, beside the hedge, under the shade of a big white umbrella. Onion tart and tomato salad, bread and cheese, a plate of dark blue figs. My aunt and uncle drank a lot of wine. They went indoors for a siesta.

I sat on, idly looking at the bushes, the flowerbeds. All sun-drenched, glittering. The shutters of the rooms upstairs were only half closed. I heard my aunt call out and laugh. Her noise rattled against my skin.

The dog Betty appeared in the farthest corner of the garden. She emerged from under the fig tree which grew there, began to toddle across the grass. She pursued her sedate, determined way as though it were marked out for her, pushing aside tall clumps of weeds that blocked her path, stepping delicately over the empty wine bottle my uncle had let fall. She didn't bother looking at me. I decided she must be on some private dog-road, some sort of dogs' short-cut via holes in our hedge we hadn't seen.

106

She flattened herself by the gate and tried to wriggle under. She was too fat to manage it. She whined and thumped her tail. I got up and opened the gate. She trotted through, then paused. She was waiting for me. I thought I would follow her to find out where she'd go.

She crossed the road and turned into the alley. Madame Cabazou's house, I knew, was the first one along. On the opposite side, on the corner with the street, was the priest's house behind its high wall. Betty didn't go home to her mistress. She nosed at a low wicker gate set into the wall near the end of the alley.

I tore aside the rusty wire netting stretched across the top of the gate and peered over it. A short path, overhung with creepers, led steeply upwards to a stone façade half obscured by leaves. I understood. This was a back way into the priest's house, one not protected by padlocks and keys. In a moment I'd climbed through the netting and over the gate and dropped down on the other side. The branches of trees brushed my face and arms. Soft debris of dead leaves under my feet. I stood still and listened. The entire village seemed to be asleep. No sharp voice, no tap on my shoulder, pulled me back. I crept up the path. I forgot Betty: she'd gone.

The house rose up before me, wide, three solid storeys of cream-coloured stone under a red-tiled roof. Blank-faced, its brown shutters closed. Three steps led up to its double wooden door. On either side of this were stone benches with claw feet, and tall bushes of oleander spilling worn pink flowers along the ground. I didn't hurry working out how to enter the house because the garden laid insistent hands on me and made me want to stay in it for ever.

From the outside you couldn't see that there was a garden at all. It was hidden. A secret place. It was small and square

107

and overgrown, completely enclosed by the towering walls that surrounded it: the house on one side, the neighbour's barn on a second, and the walls of the street and the alleyway on the other two.

Inside these walls the garden was further enclosed by a luxuriant green vine trained on to wires. What must once have been a tidy green plot edged by the vine, by bushes and trees, was now a thicket you had to push your way into. I crept into a little sweet-smelling box of wilderness. Just big enough to hold me. Just the right size. In its green heart I stood upright in the long grass and counted two cherry trees, an apple tree laden with fruit, more oleanders, a lofty bush of bamboo plumes and several of blackcurrant. I picked a leaf and rubbed it to release the harsh scent. There was an ancient well in one corner, fenced about with cobwebs and black iron spikes. I lifted its wooden lid, peered down at its black mirror, threw a pebble in and heard the far splash.

I was frightened of going into the house all by myself, so I dared myself to do it as soon as the church bells began to strike the hour. The doors were clasped together merely by a loop of thin wire. I twisted a stick in it, broke it. Then I pushed the doors open and entered the house.

Once I'd wrestled with the shutters in the kitchen and flung them wide, screeching on their unoiled hinges, I could see. The red-tiled floor, the white fireplace with columns on either side and a white carving of scrolls and flowers above, the stone arch I'd come through from the hall, the cooker black with grease, the yellow oilcloth on the table.

A corridor wound around the ground floor. I passed a store-room full of old furniture and carpentry things, a wine cellar lined with empty metal racks, a poky lavatory with decorated blue tiles going up the wall. I picked my way up an open wooden staircase, like a ladder, to the salon and the bedrooms above. The salon was empty, grand as a ballroom but desolate. Striped blue and gold wallpaper hung down in curly strips, exposing the plaster and laths behind. The floor was bendy when I walked on it. The bedrooms were dusty and dark, falls of soot piled in their fireplaces. Old stained mattresses rested on broken-down springs, old books, parched covers stiff with dirt, sprawled face down on the lino, old chairs with cracked backs and seats were mixed up anyhow with rolls of lino, split satin cushions.

I put out my hands and touched these things in the half-dark. I draped my shoulders with a torn bedspread of scarlet chenille, then passed my hands over the wounded furniture. I blessed it, I told it to be healed now, and that it was forgiven. Then I departed from those sad rooms, closing their doors behind me one by one.

I crawled up a second wooden stair, to the attic. Bright spears of light tore gaps in the walls and roof, pointed at a floor littered with feathers and droppings. A headless plaster statue leaned in the far corner. His hands clasped a missal. He wore a surplice and cassock. I recognised him, even without his head, as St John Vianney, the curé of Ars. We'd done him at school. I looked for his head among the dusty junk surrounding him but couldn't find it. So I went back downstairs, into the garden again.

My bed in our old house was in the corner of the room. Shadows fingered the wall next to me and lay down on me like blankets. You'd draped a shadow over your face like a mantilla. You advanced, carrying a night-light. I was afraid of the dark but not of you, even though a grey cobwebby mask clung to your eyes and mouth and hid them.

You bent over me and spoke.

– What a mess you've left everything in. Bits and pieces all over the place. Silly girl.

You whispered in my ear.

– One day I'll tell you all the secrets I've ever known.

My aunt ladled cold cucumber soup from the white china tureen into white soup plates. We pushed our spoons across the pale green ponds, to and fro like swimmers. My spoon was big, silver-plated; I liked its heaviness in my hand. My uncle drank his soup heartily, stuffed in mouthfuls of bread, called for a second helping. My aunt waved the ladle at the moths butting the glass dome of the lamp she'd set on the table. It threw just enough light for us to eat by. The rest of the garden was swallowed by black night. From Madame Cabazou's house across the street came the sound of a man's voice reading the news on TV.

My aunt and uncle spoke to each other and left me in peace. I could lean against their chat like a pillow while I searched my memory.

– No, my father said on the morning of the funeral: I don't believe in the afterlife. Though your mother tried to. Bound to, wasn't she, being a Catholic. We just conk out I think. That's the end of it. The end of consciousness.

My uncle's red cheeks bulged with bread. He caught my eye and lifted his glass to me. My aunt collected our empty soup plates and stacked them on one side of the table. My uncle swallowed his faceful of bread and fetched the next course. Stuffed red peppers. I lifted mine out of the dish on to my plate, inserted my knife, slit the red skin. The pepper fell apart easily, like a bag of thin red silk. Rice and mushrooms tumbled out, a strip of anchovy.

110

– Overcooked, frowned my aunt: your fault, Lily, for coming back so late. Whatever were you up to?

I shrugged and smiled.

– Oh we understand, she said: you're young, you don't want to hang around all the time with us middle-aged folks! And we trust you to be sensible. Not to do anything silly.

She began to toss green salad in a clear plastic bowl, moving the wooden spoons delicately between the oily leaves that gave off the fragrance of tarragon.

– Of course you need some time by yourself, she said: especially just now. You want to amuse yourself, spend time by yourself, that's fine. Of course we understand.

It was early evening when I arrived at the house. Climbing the hill had taken me several hours. Now the sky at the horizon was green, as sharp as apples. The moon rose. A single silver star burned high above the lavender-blue sea.

The house was built into the cliff, at the very top, where the chalky ground levelled out, became turf dotted with gorse, sea-pinks, scabious. The front door stood open so I went in.

The whole place smelt of freshly sawn wood. Fragrance of resin, of cedar. Large rooms, airy and light. The walls and ceilings were painted a clear glowing blue. Beds were dotted about, manuscripts spilled across them. I wondered who they were, the people who lived here and strewed their papers over their beds. Then I saw the figure of a woman in the far doorway, leaning against the frame of the door, with her back to me. The owner of the house. Would she mind my presence? I was uninvited. A trespasser.

She turned round.

I'd forgotten that you'd ever looked like this. Young, with thick curly brown hair, amused hazel eyes, fresh unlined

111

skin. Not a trace of sorrow or of pain. You were healthy. You were fully alive.

– I'm living here now, you explained with a smile and a wave of the hand: in Brahma's house.

You walked me about the spacious blue rooms, up and down the wide, ladder-like staircases of golden wood.

– Tell your father, you said: the cure for grief is, you have to sit by an open window and look out of it.

Your face was calm. No fear in it. You weren't suffering any more.

– You look so well, I blurted out: and all your hair's grown back!

– It's time for you to go, you told me.

You stood on the front steps and waved me off. My eyes measured the width of the doorway. I thought I'd slip through, stay with you. You shook your head, slammed the door shut on my efforts to break back in.

At eight o'clock prompt each day a siren wailed along the main road. That second morning, Madame Cabazou leaned over our gates and called.

– The bread van. Hurry up, girl. It doesn't wait long.

I stumbled after her, half-asleep. She dashed along on nimble slippered feet, a thick cardigan thrust on over her white nightdress. The dog Betty trailed us, folds of fat swaying.

Down by the fountain we joined a queue of old people who all smiled and exclaimed. Madame Cabazou introduced me, made me shake hands all round. Once I was part of them they went on swapping bits of news. Madame Cabazou was the lively one. Her chatter was staccato, her hands flew about like the swallows that zigzagged between our house and barn.

– My wretched grandchildren, she cried: they hardly ever come and see me. Children these days. Oh they don't care.

I bought a bag of croissants and a thick loaf, one up from a baguette, that was called simply a *pain*. I walked slowly back up the street to the house. The voices of the old people rose and fell behind me, bubbles of sound, like the splash of water in the fountain. They were recalling the funeral they'd been to the week before. A young girl, from a farm over by the lake, had been trapped by her hair in her father's baling machine and strangled. The voices grew high and excited, like the worrying of dogs.

After breakfast my aunt and uncle drove off in the car to visit the castle at Montségur. I waved them goodbye, then prowled about the kitchen, collecting the things I needed and packing them into a basket. I shut the grey metal gates behind me and crossed the road into the alleyway.

Madame Cabazou was working in the little vegetable patch in front of her house. Her thin body was bent double as she tugged weeds from the earth. Today she had on a blue housecoat, and she'd tied her straw hat on like a bonnet, the strings knotted under her chin. I slunk past while her stooped back was turned and hoisted myself over the wicker gate.

Once inside the priest's kitchen I opened the shutters and the windows to let in light and air. I swept the floor with the dustpan and brush I'd brought, dusted the table and the fireplace and the windowsills. I laid a fire, with sticks and bits of wood from the store-room. I'd brought a small saucepan to cook in. I had a metal fish-slice and one wooden spoon. For lunch I might have stewed apples, using the fruit from the tree outside. I might try mixing up some grape juice. I had three plastic bottles of mineral water in my basket, a croissant saved from breakfast, a blue and white checked teacloth, and a couple of books. I left all this equipment on the table in the kitchen, and went outside.

I dropped into the garden like a stone or a plant, taking up my place. The garden had been waiting for me. I belonged in it. I had discovered it and in that act had been accepted by it. Now I was part of it. Hidden, invisible. The long grass closed over my head, green water. The bushes stretched wide their flowering branches around me. The bright green vine walled me in with its jagged leaves, curling tendrils, heavy bunches of grapes. Around the edges of the garden rustled the tops of the trees.

I had plenty of time to get to know the garden. I had seven whole days in which to stare at the ants and beetles balanced on the blades of grass next to my face, to finger the different textures of stems, to listen to the crickets and birds. I rolled over on to my back, put my hands under my head, and stared at the sky through branches and leaves. My hammock. I swung in it upside down. It dandled me. I fell asleep and didn't wake for hours.

Over supper my aunt and uncle told me about the castle of Montségur, perched on top of a steep mountain. They'd climbed up the slippery rocks. They'd eaten their picnic in the lofty stronghold where the Cathars had held out against St Dominic's armies come to smash them and drag them down to the waiting pyre.

– God how I loathe the Catholic Church, cried my aunt: God how I loathe all priests!

My uncle poured red wine into tumblers.

– Nice day, Lily? he asked.

I nodded. My mouth was full of cream-laden spaghetti scented with rosemary and sage. I had the idea that if I kept on eating the memory of my mother wouldn't be able to climb out of my silence, out of the long gaps between my words, and disturb me. So I held out my plate for a second helping and bent my head over it. I concentrated on the pleasures of biting, of chewing and swallowing, the pleasure of feeling full.

I was in bed but I wasn't asleep. The room was dark, and very warm. Gold glow of a lamp in one corner. Rain beat against the window, I heard it shush-shush through the curtains. Around me was folded the softest and lightest of quilts. Like being tucked up in a cloud. Or held in your arms. For you were there, a dim presence by the lamp, humming to yourself while you read a book about gardening. Peace was the physical knowledge of warmth, of your familiar profile, your sleeve of dark pink silk resting on the plump arm of your chair, the dim blue and gold pattern of the wallpaper.

You repeated to me: you're safe now. Safe now. Safe now.

– Our last day, Lily, smiled my aunt: are you sure you don't want to come out with us for a drive? I can't think what you find to do on your own here day after day.

I shook my head.

– Well, she said: if you don't, you don't, I suppose. You could make a start on your packing, in that case.

Her words jolted me. For seven days I'd been in retreat, in my private green world. I'd ceased to hear the church bells banging out the hours overhead. Hunger was my only clock. A week, in which I'd lain on the grass reading or daydreaming, had flowed past without my knowing or caring what day it was. Back home my schoolbooks waited, and a timetable ruled into squares.

I had an ache inside me. A sort of yawn that hurt. A voice

in my stomach that wanted to scream. I felt stretched, and that I might topple over and break in two.

Back home I'd enter an empty house. My mother was dead. If only that could be a fact that was well past, something I'd dealt with and got over. Recovered from. I didn't want to embark on a life in which she'd go on and on being dead, on and on not being there. I didn't want to let it catch up with me. I shut the grey metal gates and hurried across the road.

Madame Cabazou was sitting on her front step, picking fleas out of Betty's coat. She nipped them between her fingernails until their little black backs cracked. Crack! Crack! She brushed the fleas from her fingertips like grains of black sand.

– Do you want some melons? she asked: I've got far too many. Even with this tiny patch I've grown more, this year, than I can use.

She waved her hand at the tidy rows of tomatoes, melons and courgettes. The earth between them was spotless, fine as sieved flour. She scowled at it.

– We used to have proper fields of crops, and the vineyard. Not like this. This pocket handkerchief of a garden. Oh I do miss all that, I can't tell you how much.

– Perhaps one melon? I suggested: we're leaving tomorrow morning early. We could have melon tonight.

– Come and fetch it later on, she sang out: I'll pick you one that's really ripe.

She shoved Betty's nose off her lap, and got up. She put her hands in her pockets and gazed at me.

She jerked her head towards the wicker gate in the wall.

– Some German people coming to view the house this afternoon, she remarked: with a lady from the agency.

I tried to sound indifferent.

– Oh really?

– The man who drives the bread-van told me, she said: this morning. His brother-in-law works in the café next door to the agency in Carcassonne, he heard them talking about it when they came in for a beer. Didn't you hear him say so down at the van this morning? You were off in some dream.

Coldness clutched me inside. I stared at Madame Cabazou.

– If I were you, she said: I'd come and fetch that melon this afternoon. You dream too much, it's not good. Better wake up. Otherwise you can be sure you'll be in trouble. Too much time by yourself, that's your problem.

Her words hurt me like slaps on the face. I swung away without saying anything. Tears burned my eyes but I wouldn't cry while she was watching me. I heard her front door close, then her voice drifted through the window, scolding Betty, breaking into song. She was cold-hearted. She didn't care how much she'd upset me. She didn't know how it felt to be told I'd got to leave this house and this garden for good.

I'd believed for a whole week that it was my house, my garden. I'd hardly believed it even. I just knew it. I'd just been part of it. The garden had seemed to know me, had taken me in without fuss. Leaving it, going outside and not coming back, would be like having my skin peeled off. I might die. Something was tearing me apart inside. It frightened me. I was a piece of paper being slowly ripped in two. I staggered, and fell on to the little patch of tangled grass under the vine. I started crying and could not stop. The crying went on and on, and the pain. It twisted me up, it sawed me, it squeezed my heart so I could hardly breathe. The worst thing was feeling so lonely, and knowing I always would.

Just before my mother died, the night before, I was with her. It wasn't her any more, this tiny person so thin under her nightie I couldn't bear to look at her, with clawlike hands and a head that was a skull. Her eyes were the same, that was the only part of her left that I knew. She looked out of the darkness she was in and recognised me. For a couple of minutes she fought her way up from the morphine and tried to speak. She looked at me so trustfully. My father had said I should say goodbye to her but I couldn't.

– You're not going to die just yet are you, I said loudly: you're not going to die just yet.

Her cracked lips tried to smile.

– Oh yes I am, she whispered: oh yes I think I am.

That night I dreamed of her bed in the glass conservatory, half in and half out of the house. I woke up at dawn and saw the sky like red glass. My father came in and said my mother had just died.

I could think of her being alive. I could think of her being dead. What I could not bear to think of was that moment when she died, was dying, died. When she crossed over from being alive to being dead. I couldn't join the two things up, I couldn't connect them, because at the point where they met and changed into each other was pain, my body caught in a vice, my bones twisted and wrenched, my guts torn apart. I gave birth to her dying. Violently she was pulled out of me. I felt I was dying too. I could hear an animal howling. It was me.

I lay on the grass exhausted. I felt empty. Nothing left in me. I was an old sack used then thrown away. Now I was low as the grass, low as the ground. Flattened. I was worn out. As though a mountain had stamped on me.

A yawn possessed me and I looked up. My eyelids felt swollen like car tyres, and my nose too, and my mouth. I licked the salt tears off the corners of my lips, blew my nose.

I lay staring at the gnarled trunk of the vine, the weeds and grasses stirring about its root, the yellow flowers mixed in with them whose name I didn't know.

Then it stopped being me looking at the vine, because I dissolved into it, became it. I left me behind. Human was the same as plant. This corner of the garden, the earth: one great warm breathing body that was all of us, that lived strongly, whose life I felt coursing inside me, sap blood juices of grass. Love was the force that made things grow. Love grew the vine, the weeds, me. I started crying again because of the joy. It swept through me. The knowledge of love. Such sweetness and warmth inside me and the vine and the grass under the light of the sun.

Madame Cabazou whistled for me as though I were Betty. We both came running. I carried a melon home under each arm. She kissed me on both cheeks to say goodbye, instructed me, if I wished to be well thought of, to write to her. She snatched me out of my garden, shook me, set me upright, told me to go home now. She pushed me off.

Next morning I slumped in the back seat of the car as we drove out of the village and headed for the motorway. I wanted to take the road back, to go the other way, to stay. I cried as we left the high golden hills and descended on to the plain. The wind from the sea, that Madame Cabazou called the *marin*, blew strongly. It meant the end of summer. It sang an elegy for my mother. She was dead she was gone I had lost her she would never come back and live with us again.

Every cell in every leaf had had a voice, which spoke to me.

– Of course I am here. Where else should I be but here. Where else could I possibly be.

LAUNDRY

Once upon a time, long ago, there was a woodcutter living with his wife in their ancient and ramshackle cottage of plaster and wattle on the outskirts of the great forest of Jumièges by the river Seine in Normandy. The forest was a gloomy place, particularly in winter, when its paths were icy and almost impassable, and certainly too forbidding and dark to venture down alone. Summer and winter, however, the woodcutter worked in the forest, for he had four children to feed. His wife, besides keeping house, tended the vegetable patch, looked after their cow and hens, and took butter and eggs to sell in the local market. They scratched a living, just about, despite the high rent they had to pay their landlords, the monks of Jumièges abbey, and they did not hope for anything more. When it rained, as it frequently did, they tramped about their work with sacks over their heads. When the trodden earth floor of the cottage turned to mud they put planks across it and just got on with things. When the roof leaked, and rain fell on their beds, they simply moved the beds out of the way and set buckets to catch the drips.

The daughter of the family, who was named Austreberthe, was, however, a complainer. When the washing froze to the line and turned into stiff boards, glazed with silvery ice that skinned her fingertips raw, she whinged. When the harsh soda she used on washing day stung her cracked hands, she cried out. When her chilblains bled when she forced her sabots on in the mornings, she wept.

– Don't go on so, the woman would warn her cross daughter: or the wild boars in the forest will get you and gobble you up!

At these moments Austreberthe looked even plainer than usual. Even on her good days she could not be called pretty. Her ears stuck out, her hair was mouse-coloured and refused to curl, and she was small and thin.

– You're so ugly and loud-mouthed, her three elder brothers scolded her: how will you ever find a husband?

– I'll do my best for you, sighed her father: but I have no dowry to give you.

– What on earth, asked her mother: will become of you?

In the year that Austreberthe turned sixteen, the weather was unusually fine. No late frosts spoiled the spring planting of vegetables or blighted the fruit trees. Throughout April and May the orchards of Jumièges were thick with pink blossom. Buds fattened and swelled, green leaves burst out. The sunshine of June and July transformed the forest, dappling it with light. The paths became inviting, edged with fresh green ferns and alive with birds.

Early in the morning of what promised to be an especially warm and cloudless August day, Austreberthe played truant. Instead of mucking out the cowshed, as she'd been told to do, she seized a basket, shouted to her mother that she was off to search for mushrooms, and ran into the forest. She made for one of her favourite places: a clearing where the track ran alongside a stream. Dropping her basket, she stripped off her clothes and stepped down into the water, using her cupped hands as a scoop to pour water over herself. Then she clambered out and lay stark naked on the grass in the hot sunshine.

Clip-clop. Clip-clop.

Austreberthe was roused from her daydream. She leapt up, grabbed her clothes, and ran with them to the edge of the clearing. She hurled herself full-length in the long grass behind a clump of beech trees, where she could not be seen. Then, parting the sweet-smelling stems waving to and fro just an inch from her face, she peered out of her hiding-place.

A little grey donkey trotted into view, laden with two large wicker panniers. Behind him strolled a hefty youth dressed in a monk's woollen robe. The hood of his habit was thrown back, letting the sun glint on his tonsured head. His sleeves were rolled up over long graceful arms downy with blond hairs, and his skirts were kilted about his knees, affording Austreberthe an excellent view of his fine muscular legs. He drove the heavily burdened donkey along in front of him, rhythmically switching it on the rump to keep it ambling at a steady pace, and he whistled loudly through his strong white teeth. His eyes were bright blue, his nose aquiline, and his pursed mouth rosy and plump.

Austreberthe whistled back to him, in a mocking echo of his song.

The young monk jumped and turned round.

– Who's that? he cried: who's there?

Austreberthe flattened herself even further among the grasses, her head turned aside and pillowed on moss, and whistled again.

The monk's attention was fairly caught. He stood stock still in the centre of the path and scratched his shining shaved head, tugged at the scrap of blond fringe that encircled it. The donkey seized his chance and bolted, the panniers bumping up and down on his grey flanks. The monk let loose a string of curses, dropped his stick, and raced after the fleeing ass. Austreberthe rolled over, laughing, in the long grass. Her outflung hand knocked against something porous and white, which broke and fell over. It was one of the largest wild mushrooms she'd ever seen. Several more were growing close by. She picked them and put them in her basket. Then she flung on her clothes and went home. The mushrooms saved her from the beating she would otherwise undoubtedly have received from her exasperated mother. Instead she was given a hearty clap on the shoulder.

– I'll take them to market tomorrow and sell them, her mother said: they'll fetch a good price, these lovelies, such big ones, and such a labour to find.

Next day, as was her weekly custom, Austreberthe's mother took the eggs she'd collected from her hens, the slab of butter she'd made from the creamy milk of her cow, and packed them into a basket, laying the dark, fragrant mushrooms carefully on top, and covering the whole with a clean white cloth. Then she set off for Pavilly, the large village at the other end of the forest from Jumièges, which boasted, besides its fair-sized market-place and parish church, a convent of nuns famous for making the best calvados and the best spiced honeybread for miles around.

She returned home that afternoon with an empty basket and a full purse, and a tiny flask of calvados in her pocket. She sprinkled a few drops of this on the apple pancakes she cooked for supper, and drank the rest of it with her husband as they all sat around the fire afterwards. A fire on a summer evening was a great treat, tots of calvados an almost unheard-of luxury. Austreberthe looked at her parents with suspicion.

– The cellaress of the convent came down to market, her mother said: she bought all my mushrooms for the prioress's dinner, she gave me this calvados, and she told me the convent badly needs a lay sister or two to serve as washerwomen. The monks of Jumièges have elected a new Abbot, who insists that the monks bath every week and regularly wear clean underclothes. So they have started sending all their laundry to Pavilly for the nuns to wash, and the poor sisters are run off their feet with it. They don't like to refuse their dear brothers in Christ this help, but they're at their wits' end to know how to manage. Well, they *were*, until I told the cellaress my idea.

Austreberthe's mother looked triumphantly at her daughter.

– You, my dear child, are going to enter the convent at Pavilly as a lay sister and become washerwoman to the nuns. It's the work of God's grace. It solves everything.

Her three brothers whooped with laughter.

– You'll have to learn some manners now, they cried: you'll have to learn to be quiet now!

– Who knows, said her father: you might even become a saint!

– What about a dowry? asked Austreberthe: I thought nuns had to have dowries?

– The cellaress agreed, replied her mother: that your house-wifely skills will do very well instead.

She drained the last of her calvados from her tiny earthenware cup, and yawned.

– The cellaress told me, she remarked: that the poor young monk who brings the laundry over to the convent got attacked in the forest yesterday. A wild boar, he said it was.

– Really? asked Austreberthe.

– Apparently, went on her mother: he saw something leaping in the long grass, with a bristly brown back. Then it charged him, so he had to run away. The donkey carrying the dirty washing bolted, and the panniers fell off, and everything ended up wet and muddy in the stream. The young man was so upset that the nuns had to feed him slices of honeybread to cheer him up. Of course it wasn't his fault. No one would dream of punishing him. But just fancy! A wild boar in that part of the forest, so near to our home!

– How fortunate, remarked Austreberthe: that it was the dirty washing that fell into the stream and not the clean!

She entered the convent a week later, taking gifts for the nuns of eggs, butter and more mushrooms. The cellaress received her kindly, kissing her on both cheeks and setting a plate of the famous spiced honeybread in front of her, and with her own hands dressing Austreberthe in her new habit, cutting off her hair with a large pair of shears, and showing her how to pin the white linen veil over her close-fitting coif.

– Try not to get your clothes too dirty, warned the cellaress: even with all the rough work you have to do you can't be having clean aprons and habits all the time. That would lead to the sin of vanity. And please remember that *we*, unlike our dear brothers in Christ at Jumièges, bathe only twice a year, at Christmas and at Easter, lest we fall into the sin of impurity, in thought at least if not in deed!

Austreberthe nodded. With the hair she disliked cut off, and the sticking-out ears that so distressed her concealed, she felt cheerful. She was ready for business. She set to immediately in the wash-house, sorting out the great heap of wet and muddy laundry that had arrived a week ago from Jumièges, after its dousing in the stream, and had not yet been dealt with.

There were, it seemed to her, a hundred pairs at least of long underpants in heavy unbleached wool. These, clearly, belonged to the monks. The Abbot's drawers, however, were of the finest white linen, with tiny tucks and pleats, and Austreberthe admired them very much. She stoked up the fire under the copper in the back scullery, then soaked and washed and scrubbed and scoured and rinsed and wrung until her body streamed with sweat and ached with exhaustion. But Austreberthe did not complain. She carried the washing outside and hung it to dry in the orchard, looping it from branch to branch of the apple trees and spreading it on the hedges behind. Next day she pressed it with a heated flat-iron, and then packed it, interleaved with sprigs of lavender and rosemary, into panniers ready for collection. Then, having first made sure the other nuns were not around, she stripped off her habit and veil and washed herself all over under the pump in the back yard.

Since her own drawers were still damp with sweat from her labours of the day before, and she wouldn't be allowed a clean pair till Christmas, she tossed them aside. Then she dressed herself again, very carefully, in her habit and veil.

Clip-clop. Clip-clop.

The donkey's hooves rang on the cobbles of the convent yard. The young monk came into the damp, steamy wash-house, his blue eyes modestly cast down and the corners of his plump red lips turned up, his graceful arms hidden in

127

his sleeves. He inclined his head to the young lay sister, who nodded back.

– Bring in the washing, then, she directed him: I'm ready for you.

Her voice, as befitted the inhabitant of such a holy place as a convent, was pitched very low. Its contralto note sounded tuneful and sweet as the whistle of a bird. The young monk raised his eyes shyly to Austreberthe's smiling face, so becomingly framed in her white coif.

– We're grateful to you, dear sister, he stammered: for the service that you do us.

He picked up the two baskets of clean washing and carried them outside. Then he brought in the baskets of dirty washing and set them on the stone floor.

– A slice of honeybread before you go? suggested Austreberthe: a tot of calvados? You've a long journey ahead of you through the forest. You must keep up your strength. And while you refresh yourself I'll just finish ironing the Abbot's drawers for you to take back with you.

She guided the young monk into the back scullery where the flat-irons were set at the edge of the stove, and shut the door behind them. In here it was quite dark. The room was warm. It smelt of lavender soap and sun-dried linen, as sweet as grass.

Austreberthe gave a cry and pointed.

– Over there. In the corner. A wild boar!

She clutched at the young monk and fell over backwards with him on to a heap of nuns' nightdresses and wimples.

– A wild boar? shouted the monk: in here? Don't be ridiculous!

Austreberthe flung back the skirts of her habit.

– Look, she cried: all brown and bristly.

She held tightly to the young monk so that he could not run away. Her skin seemed scented with the tang of wild mushrooms. Her mouth, close to his, tasted of honey and apples.

– Though some, she murmured: would not say bristly but silky soft. Brown and curly. Wouldn't you?

Some time later, the little grey donkey, laden with its panniers of clean washing, galloped back through the forest of Jumièges towards the monastery, the young monk running behind and lashing the poor beast's rump with great force while whistling a cheerful hymn. Every week after that he set out again for the convent at Pavilly, with the donkey and the panniers of washing, and his brothers in Christ greatly praised him for traversing the forest so fearlessly despite the frequent encounters he reported with the bristly brown boar.

As for Sister Austreberthe, such was her piety, wit and intelligence that she was quickly promoted to the position of Bursar and thence to that of Mistress of Novices. For her humility in insisting on continuing to do the monks' laundry, even after her elevation, in later years, to the lofty rank of Prioress, she was revered as the holiest of nuns. After her death she was canonised, and made patroness of the forest of Jumièges. Many stories are told about Saint Austreberthe, though not this one, you may be sure.

UNE GLOSSAIRE/
A GLOSSARY

ABSENCE

My childhood in France is vanishing, a tide going out. Each day, the receding waters stretch further away. Each day, the incoming tide reaches less high up the beach. The absent sea scrawls a memoir behind itself along the tideline, written in seaweed, driftwood, dead starfish, broken glass bottles, fragments of cork. I want to collect up this debris, decipher it, before the sea returns and obliterates it. I need to keep coming back to this seashore at Etretat in Normandy, to walk along the tideline and re-examine these mysterious traces, this line of fluid script, this low-water mark dividing the pebbles from the shingle; to reselect and rearrange.

As a child I dream frequently of being erased by the sea. I

walk along the beach, the high sea-wall beside me, and watch the violent waves crash over the rocks. The sea advances up the beach, more and more stormy, and I back away until, the wall behind me, there is nowhere left to go. Then the sea flops over my head and swallows me.

My grandmother has already vanished. She died in 1979. For the first few years after her death her absence is marked through her place laid at table for every meal: knife, fork, spoon, plate, glass, silver napkin ring. Then that custom dies, that trace eradicated. The arrangements of the house – furniture, mealtimes – remain the same, and testify to her memory. I find her on the kitchen shelves, upright as the blue and white jars marked *farine* and *épices*. I find her laid away, tidy and fragrant, in the big carved cupboard in her bedroom where her wedding sheets, thick linen with drawn-thread work along the top edge and her monogram in the corner, are folded in boxes between layers of tissue-paper.

My grandfather has had a heart attack, and two strokes. He lives imprisoned in his chair, his speech thickened and blurred. He's over ninety. How much longer has he got? He clutches the edge of the cliff: the sea lies below, waiting for him.

My aunt, who takes the main responsibility for looking after him in addition to working full-time, now has breast cancer. She is receiving chemotherapy treatment. Next month (February 1986) she will have a mastectomy. She pits herself against the incoming tide, hands flung out in protest: not yet.

Each day, the debris of memories scattered along the rise of the beach is a little different: new arrangements of shells, torn bits of plastic, broken lobster baskets, lumps of tar. In the past, when I have written about my childhood, one of my sisters or my mother has complained: that's not true; it wasn't like that; you've made it up. Yes, I'm making it up: I'm putting it back together again. I'm walking along the beach, staring at the prospect of the death of the grandfather and aunt I love; of their final absence; of my final separation from my childhood structured in their house. Into the face of this loss I cast my words, pebbles thrown into the sea. I'm going to write a sort of geography. To reclaim the past. The waves race backwards through my fingers, and I can't hold on to them. I lick the salt on my hands, and set myself to remembering.

ARTICHAUTS

Artichokes. Big, fat and green, with closely packed pointed leaves. The inside ones are violet, almost transparent. We eat them, boiled, for supper, pulling off the leaves one by one and dipping them into hot cream before scraping them between our teeth. The heart is the best, mashed up in the cream. Grandpère eats them with vinaigrette.

ASSOMPTION

Assumption. The feast-day of the village is the fifteenth of August, the feast of the Assumption of the Virgin Mary into heaven.

At six o'clock in the morning, we are woken by the boom of cannon fired in the playing field on the Goderville road. My mother brings us an early cup of tea, for we must fast from liquid for three hours before receiving Holy Communion, and from food from midnight.

We dress in our smartest clothes. Cotton dress, navy cropped blazer with brass buttons, white socks, well-polished shoes. At ten o'clock, the bells begin to ring, summoning us to High Mass. We gather in the hall. Waiting for the others,

I study the large framed engraving of Theseus bearing off Hyppolita, Queen of the Amazons, to be his bride. She takes it calmly, sitting upright in his chariot, bare massive arms lifted to adjust the transparent veil falling across her face. A stand topped with black marble bears flowering plants, brass candlesticks and dishes, a bronze sculpture of a tiger. I never tire of pulling my fingers along his cold hard upraised tail. White gloves are donned. Missals with gilt clasps are taken up. Grandpère twirls his stick. We are off.

The verger has a red face and black moustaches and wears a braided frockcoat with epaulettes and military medals. He motions us into the church. All through High Mass he knocks his decorated staff fiercely on the ground to tell us to rise, kneel, sit. The vast church is choked with people. Waiting. Then, far off in the distance, we hear the crashing jangly music of the village brass band marching up, up, through the great doors and along the aisle to their special place at the front, a ragged procession of serious men and boys in brown uniforms bearing their great gleaming instruments. They play at special moments all through Mass. At the Consecration and Elevation of the Host, the bells peal out, the organ booms, and the band roars and trumpets. Aged priests weighted down in gold brocade copes, half hidden by clouds of incense, the sweet smoke. Bouquets of white flowers around the altar and side altars at the feet of the saints, suspended from the tall columns. The village widows in black frocks, black bonnets and veils, black misshapen shoes. Everyone in their best clothes. After Mass, the band processes out, playing a sacred cacophony, and we follow them to the cemetery, where we stand in silence to honour the dead of two world wars.

Lunch. The table is extended with extra wooden leaves, to run the full length of the salon, and is draped with thick, gleaming white tablecloths on which shine silver and glass, arrangements of flowers. While the guests are sipping their *apéritifs* in Grandmère's bedroom, transformed into a little *salon*, a gang of women gathers in the kitchen to peel the freshly cooked potatoes. I feel like an adult, received into this bevy of aunts talking and laughing as their deft knives rapidly lift off the hot skins. The kitchen is the sanctuary, the tabernacle of the women, where the superlative feast is prepared by their hands alone, while the men talk to the priest next door.

One dish slowly succeeds another. The noise of conversation washes up and down the long table, eddies upwards from the flat basket of peaches and grapes and plums arranged on scarlet leaves. We're too excited to feel bored. Pale yellow ice-cream released from its tall copper mould. Coffee in tiny gold-rimmed cups. Chocolates. Calvados and cognac and Bénédictine.

At three o'clock we go down to the village to watch the procession, finding a good place to stand: high up on a grassy bank at the crossroads. The carts, drawn by tractors, grinning youths perched high up at the wheel, are entirely covered in paper flowers, in pink or white or pale blue, and are decorated to represent different scenes of country life. Little children are animals. Older ones are giggling flower maidens and swains. Lastly comes the Queen of the day: the local village beauty with her attendants, all got up in satin and flowers, like a bride, a gilt tiara anchored to her beehive hairdo, white satin stilettos on her big feet. We're puzzled as to why she's been chosen: her face is hard and red, her eyes small, her hair crimped and frizzy. Not so is Brigitte Bardot. But she's indisputably female, with her plump bosom and calves, her tossing head, her languishing smile. How can I ever become a woman? This one frightens me. Her sexuality frightens me, though I don't have a word for it.

135

We go on to the fair, which has been set up in the big field beyond the church. Carnival atmosphere: the normal social relations of the village turn topsy-turvy as the country people swagger arm in arm, in gangs, laughing boisterously, swarming in from their farms to take over the space, enjoy themselves freely, not bother with politeness and decorum. I'm enchanted and scared. We don't matter. Our genteel world shatters. Nobody cares that we are the much-respected Caulle family. We don't know all these people's names, and they don't know ours, and they don't give a damn. We go on the round-abouts, rocking on horses and trains and cars; we throw hoops for goldfish; my brother and father shoot air-rifles. Racks of gaudy dolls dressed in tinsel and taffeta stare down at us. The women running the booths shout in hoarse voices, hands on their silken hips, cigarettes dangling. A neighbouring farmer, Gérard Le Forestier, very handsome with his black hair and ruddy face, very masculine in his severe dark overcoat, whirls me away from my parents and into the dangerous thrills and spins of the bumper-cars, on to the skidding shiny floor where men and youths drive at us, yelling in patois, around the rink decorated with crudely painted panels showing curly-haired peasant boys fondling girls with enormous pointed breasts bursting through their tight bodices. I'm outside my strictly loving and protective family. At the age of eleven, for the first time. Driving, hard and furious, with a man. Wanting to be beautiful and grown-up, to be kissed. With my shiny face and frizzy hair and white ankle socks.

In the evening, after supper, the excitement still pours and tingles. We stand in the darkness, feet planted in puddles and mud, in the field off the Goderville road, waiting for the *feux d'artifice*, the fireworks, to start. This is part of the drama: to stand next to faceless strangers in the night, to see the spurt of a match as a cigarette is lit, to be out in the village so late, to be part of the eager crowd. Then the first rocket goes up, breaking and dissolving high above our heads into gold and silver flowers, and a roaring sigh comes out with one breath from all of us together. Fountains sizzle and leap; catherine wheels jerk and then flare into whirling circles of flaming light; there is the marvellous acrid smell of chemicals, sour burning, in our nostrils. Each of the exploding rockets takes off inside me, each of those staffs of intensity rises up inside me and bursts me into a shower of golden tongues, and I cry out along with the groaning crowd.

The feast of the Assumption celebrates the fact that the Virgin Mary, at her death, rises into the sky, only faintly assisted by angels, and shoots bodily up into heaven where she is crowned Queen. I understand that, watching these fireworks. I doubt it, looking at the simpering plaster statue of Victorian piety and submission in the church. What happened to Grandmère when she died? What will happen to Brigitte? I'll never see that firework display again, yet the fiery virgin rises again and again, every year, in the muddy field. I'd like to believe she is rising inside me. I'd like to believe that death does not extinguish those I love, that they will rise up inside me as bright as rockets and explode into my mind, these words I write. The smell of cordite, of burning. The radiance fades against the black sky, and after a few seconds you wouldn't know that it's ever been there. We troop home, through the dark village, to bed.

BEURRE

Butter. Butter comes in a kilo block, wrapped in white greaseproof paper printed with a design, in blue, of cows grazing, and the name, in swirly blue letters, of the local farm which has produced it. Butter is very expensive. We are not supposed to spread it on bread at meals (except at breakfast), though my father always does and then gets into trouble because he likes his butter thick. For tea we eat *tartines* of bread and jam. I remember at a certain point having a craving for salted butter, and my mother buying it for me in tins.

BONNETIÈRE

Bonnetière. A tall, narrow cupboard, its upper half set with a glass pane, window into the interior. Here are displayed silver boxes and baskets, a massive old fan, an ivory eggcup and spoon, a gold mesh purse, old velvet-framed photographs.

My mother has brought bits of France with her into England. She has a *bonnetière* too, and she keeps her treasures in it. We're allowed to touch; to open the door and see what's inside.

BRIGITTE

Brigitte. My aunt's name. Also my middle name: as her godchild, I am named after her. I like this special relationship I have with her. I can lay hands on her, claiming her not just as aunt but as something more. She is my *marraine*. In my missal, at the place where it falls open for the order of Mass, I keep the holy picture she gives me to celebrate my First Communion in June 1957: *le petit Samuel* (Reynolds), looking just like a girl. This is me: a girl-boy, praying, in a white nightie, a bit of a prig. Brigitte also gives me a reproduction of a Virgin and Child by Raphael, in a gilded wooden frame, just like a real oil painting. I choose it myself, in the shop in Le Havre, and this is a real pleasure: to be allowed to scan all the Botticellis and to reject them, to go for the serene grave Madonna by Raphael. I've been given the image of womanhood. My own mother looks out from the gold frame at me. I'll never be able to become like her. An impossibility. I shan't be a mother. I don't know why. Thirty years later I'm longing for my own child, and I'm discovering all the bits of me not represented in the holy picture. Grandpère says to me: *Dépêche-toi de produire ton premier enfant. Je voudrais le voir avant de mourir.*

Brigitte does not marry and have children. She chooses not to. How much can she choose? How free is she? What are her options? Unmarried, she is certainly not allowed a lover, male or female. Unthinkable. The English word *spinster* gives no clue to her power, her gaiety, her air of eternal youth. Outside the house she is Mademoiselle Caulle, respected in the village both as the daughter of her parents and as herself.

Monique, my mother, is the oldest child. After university she comes abroad, to Dolgelley in Wales, where she works as the French *assistante* in Dr Williams's School for Girls. War breaks out. She meets my father, who is in the army, stationed near the school. They decide to marry. My mother tells me how happy she is to have married an Englishman. She has left home. Broken free. She returns to visit her parents and sister every year, for a long summer holiday, taking us all with her. My father comes for a fortnight, and then has to go back to his job as sales manager for the Tan-Sad Chair Company.

Bernard is the second child. My godfather. He marries Anne-Marie Spriet, whose family (the Spriets have fourteen children, of whom seven survive) live just two kilometres away on a big farm, and are old friends of the Caulles. Bernard too leaves home. His job, working for a dairy firm, takes him south, to Rodez. He introduces chocolate yoghurt into France, also a delicious confection called *Campagnard*: cream cheese overlaid with thick fresh cream. Bernard is handsome, youthful: dark eyes, thick dark brown hair, aquiline nose, a smile. His vitality makes him very attractive. He gives me an image of male sexuality (of course I don't call it that then) that means: kindness, having fun, liking women and girls. All the young men of the family he has married into are like that.

Brigitte is the youngest. Secretly we hope that she will marry Charles Spriet, our favourite; the funniest and wildest of the boys; always willing to take us around the farm and play with us. But Charles brings home a bride who is robust, loudly cheerful, *very* sexy; and Brigitte doesn't really approve of her, kind and generous as Monique (same name as my mother) is. Brigitte places great store on behaving *comme il faut* when necessary, and Monique does not even know she is breaking the rules.

One suitor arrives for Brigitte. One day we're told that there's a gentleman coming to tea, and that we're to behave just as though nothing special is happening, just to be polite. He's nervous, correct, *old*. Brigitte spends the following day sitting in the car (the only place where she can find some privacy and not be overheard) outside the house, talking it over with my mother. In the end she rejects him. He only wants a housekeeper, she says: not a real wife.

My earliest memory of Brigitte. We are living in a council house on an estate in Edgware. The railway line runs along the bottom of the garden. The milkman comes round with his horse and cart. We run out to feed sugar-lumps to the horse. I'm perhaps three years old. Then we see Brigitte running along the street towards us, her face smiling, her dark plaits twisted around her head, the skirts of her waisted coat flying out behind her, a pile of books toppling out of her arms.

Brigitte does not grow old. Perhaps that is the secret: to stay with your parents, to remain in the house of your childhood, having survived the planes bombing your back garden and the surrounding fields during the Occupation, to cling to your home and your childhood, your inheritance, and to protect it fiercely. Brigitte becomes, even more than my grandparents, the keeper of the house; the keeper of the old ways. Changes are dangerous.

As Grandmère sickens and grows more fragile and moves towards her dying, Brigitte cares for her. The mother become the child. Arranging Grandmère's cardigan and shawl, prompting her to eat, to drink, to rest, arranging her spectacles and book within reach, taking her breakfast in bed and perching on the end of the bed to talk to her. We peer through the crack in the door and glimpse their intimacy that I sometimes feel shuts my mother out. Brigitte does the same with Grandpère. A loving bossiness. He is her baby now, and she feeds him. The powerful parents under the control of their youngest child. I think there is a certain satisfaction, even a pleasurable revenge, in all this. It's also extremely hard work.

Brigitte is: energy. She's small and dark and determined, her long narrow feet leaping in tennis shoes around the house and garden, or shod for more formal occasions in elegant leather high-heels. She runs, she jumps up and down, she plays tennis, she swims, she walks. Her body in its red swimsuit is firm, ageless. She has good legs. White skin, that browns rapidly in summer, like my mother's.

It's charming, to know my mother has a sister, someone she's known for longer than she's known us, to match the two together and mark their differences, to see my mother as a woman not just as my mother, to wonder how they've each become themselves. Brigitte criticises Mum for her French accent, less pure than formerly, weighted with English sounds. She criticises Mum for abandoning France and the family, despite the fact that Mum returns every year. She's critical of married people, of men. There are no eligible men in the neighbourhood for her to marry.

She's a wonderful aunt. She plays with us, a child herself. She fetches down from the *grenier* her old toys, and shares them with us. The doll's made by Grandpère, furniture tiny hand-carved wardrobes, chairs, beds. Brigitte's doll has a trousseau of hand-sewn clothes: a severely cut winter coat, little blouses with pleats, square shoulders, yokes, dresses with collars and cuffs and tiny buttons. Grandpère has made the doll a pair of fur boots, with wooden soles. The doll has a stove, a real one, on which we cook windfalls in fragile aluminium pans. We don't want our lunch; we want to eat with the doll, who is Brigitte, who has been given the house as her own.

We play with the doll in Brigitte's bedroom, a tidy, spotless sanctum we may only enter when invited to do so. It's an enchantment to penetrate this enclosed world which is all Brigitte's own, shared with no man, to move across the polished floor of golden wood, to see the curtain on its brass rod that divides off her washstand, to spot her gold ring lying next to the soap-dish, to see yesterday's silken petticoat and stockings flung across a hanger, to consider the rack of dresses carefully hung inside the built-in cupboard under the eaves. You discover a person by these traces, the way they arrange the brass pots of cacti, the bronze busts and figures on the little antique chest of drawers, the way the pillows on the bed wear daytime covers of fine white cotton decorated with cut embroidered ovals and white ribbon, the way that treasures are carefully placed along the carved brackets above the bed. A grown-up person's things, which we are occasionally allowed to handle. No dust. Each prized object in its exact place. Touch cautiously, lest the china mouse drops, and breaks. The panelled wooden walls bear pictures, a couple of green plants trailing down. The low spreading armchair has a fat seat of worn velvet, curled claw feet. The old oblong mirror, set into an ornate gold frame, hangs above the little writing-table with its appurtenances of glass, marble, gilt. Brigitte's missal; her rosary; the crucifix above her bed, threaded with a sprig of palm from the Holy Land. In here we're hushed and tamed. Coming out on to the little landing, we enter a noisier, more ordinary world.

We don't call her aunt. She's Beewee. Or, in other moods, Tante Octavie. Meaning all that she's not: a severe person in a mob cap and spectacles, a stuff gown. (One night we leave an effigy of Tante Octavie in Brigitte's room; she dons the costume and comes to haunt us.) Brigitte wears *salopettes*, sawn-off dungarees in pink and white candy seersucker stripes. She gardens in these, squatting next to her osier basket which she rapidly fills with weeds, or she perches on the kitchen doorstep after Sunday High Mass, having changed out of her elegant dress and jacket, and shows us how to churn the ice-cream and pack the revolving drum with ice. She picks up a hammer and a thick nail and smashes up the great lump of ice on its bed of coarse grey sacking.

Brigitte has a great friend, Odile, who used to be a Carmelite novice, but who has had to leave the convent because her health is too delicate for the rigorous life. I loved the convent, she tells me: we used to laugh all day long. I blink, unable to imagine this. I want to become a nun too, but I hadn't thought the life included laughter. Brigitte and Odile sit in the veranda together, talking and sewing, listening to records, singing songs. They set off in Brigitte's grey *deux-chevaux* for walking holidays. This car is called Cocotte. Her seats are slung on thick rubber bands, and bounce wonderfully as the little car spurts along. The gear lever has to be waggled, pushed and pulled. The engine starting up makes a coughing whine.

I hang around Brigitte and Odile. Two unmarried women who are close friends. This is something new and fascinating, a way of being that does not fit into the tidy marital houses of the London suburb where we live. Odile is tall and thin, always laughing and cracking jokes. One Easter her new spring outfit is a suit in coarse navy linen, a navy hat, high-heels. She looks wonderful. She wobbles down the rough road to church in her high-heels, laughing at their absurdity.

Then Odile gets married and moves away. She and Brigitte remain friends, but it's not the same, I can see that. You have to put your husband and children first. A woman friend takes second place.

Brigitte finds another friend, younger, less fun. Edith. She makes do with what she can get. One summer the three of us go off in Cocotte for a walking holiday in Bourgogne. I'm thrilled that I've entered the category of Brigitte's friends for holidays, even though I'm only thirteen. We walk from monastery to monastery, looping back to the car at night. We eat picnics on the hillsides; cheeses bought from the monks, bread and *saucisson*. Or we make a fire over which we boil tins of *petits pois*, or *macédoine de légumes*, with eggs dropped in and poached along with the vegetables. At night we sleep in cheap small hotels. In Vézelay our ground-floor room opens on to a little walled garden, a pretty wilderness of overgrown flowerbeds and clambering vines. At night, at Brigitte's suggestion, we

144

say our prayers together, aloud. We salute the Virgin. The *patronne* of the hotel does not like us, because at night, rather than eat in the hotel restaurant, which is too expensive, we lock our door and cook ourselves supper over the camping gas. The *patronne* bangs on the door, yelling to us: *C'est défendu! c'est défendu!* Brigitte yells back to leave us alone, we're getting ready for bed. On the morning of our departure, the *patronne* chases Cocotte all down the narrow little street, screaming that we've stolen a face-flannel. I remember the scoured white spaces of the interior of Vézelay, the capitals of Autun, the *hospice* at Beaune. I remember toiling up the hot hillsides looking for Roman ruins, for flowers, for mushrooms. I remember Edith constantly giggling, constantly brushing her hair. I remember Brigitte leaping over streams, striding along, her long arms swinging.

Brigitte teaches childcare, cookery, household management and nursery nursing, to young women, in the equivalent of our technical colleges. Her subject is a science. She knows all about the exact temperatures for bathing babies, the exact amounts of flour and butter for making puff pastry, the exact proportions of a properly balanced diet. Moderation, she instructions us, frowning at my oblivious father plastering his bread with butter.

One Saturday we visit her school at Le Trait, an old mansion set among terraced gardens high up on a hillside outside Rouen. The top floors are used for the school. We see the kitchen-laboratories, the lecture halls, the demonstration rooms. We play with the doll-babies, heavy and real despite their sacking bodies. Their flopping heads convince us. It's a wild day, winds shaking raindrops from the trees in the jungly gardens we are allowed to explore and to get lost in, enormous orange slugs, their fat bodies swollen and glistening, gliding

145

towards us along the paths. The cellars of the old house yield puzzles and secrets: theatrical props and costumes; the toys of adults. We try on gold paper crowns, purple satin robes, hold wooden sceptres.

Brigitte does all the decorations for the various seasonal festivals of the Church. She arranges the flowers every week, graciously allowing the other ladies of the village to help her. She collects pine-cones, dries grasses and the flat silvery discs of honesty that she calls *la monnaie du Pape*. At harvest time she takes us gleaning. With the permission of the farmers, we cut big armfuls of corn from the edges of the fields and carry them home, where Brigitte plaits and twists them into fantastic pagan shapes and paints them gold. Then she hangs them from the columns in church for the day of the harvest festival. She plants the feminine symbols of fertility and fruitfulness in the church. She makes the church her house.

My mother's birthday is in July. Brigitte makes her a cake in the shape of a bucket, from whose open lid spill out mushrooms made from meringues. The adults are sitting in the veranda, waiting for *le dessert*. Brigitte forms us children into a procession, and we walk in through the house from the kitchen, Jackie carrying the cake and the rest of us bearing great blue hydrangeas and singing 'Happy Birthday'. Another of Brigitte's famous cakes is the great bell, of delicate sponge sandwiched and entirely coated in thick black chocolate, that she makes every year to celebrate Easter. Or she makes *gâteau de Savoie*, or a *Savarin*, or a *Diplomate*. She is the scientist in the kitchen. We are allowed to help her, so long as we obey her instructions exactly. Anything less would ruin the finished product. She is ruthless and strict, and we are honoured to be her assistants.

When I go to visit her and Grandpère, she cooks me all my

favourite meals, of which I must eat several helpings: *moules marinière*, calves' liver with onions and cognac, *artichauts à la crème*, sausages of pure pork with lentils, salt cod with cream sauce. The present is full of pain and change. We concoct these timeless meals to keep it at bay; we reminisce. Brigitte remembers all the details of our childhood. Remembering, she is young again. Carefree. The past is the best time, she insists. Young people today want to tear down all she holds most dear. Feminists are trying to destroy the family, are encouraging women to murder their unborn children, to go shouting in the streets about sex. Workers are no longer loyal to their bosses but go on strike. A socialist government has taken over in France. Married women are taking the jobs, for mere pin-money, that single women like Brigitte really need in order to earn a living. Teachers are no longer respected. Modern children are greedy and lazy and materialistic.

Such a breakdown. Such bitterness in Brigitte's voice. To enter her house, to love her, I have to leave behind the adult in me who is feminist and socialist.

– Brigitte has an awful lot to bear, my mother counsels me: don't provoke her or argue. It's best not to answer back. Just be careful what you say.

Brigitte has grown her hair long. The bulky chignon at the back of her head, which suits her, is streaked with grey. She sews at her Normandy costume, every inch of which she makes by hand: the gathered skirt, the embroidered bodice, the frilled muslin apron, the wired gauze bonnet with its two long frilled streamers, the petticoats. Once a week she indulges herself, goes out dancing with her troupe, performs the ancient dances of the countryside, summons the order and dignity of the past by moving through complex figures, feet leaping in quick patterns. She models the costume for me in the garden,

147

moving lightly, proudly, across the grass. She poses, smiling. She stands for tradition, for a dangerous dream. No black faces here. The chickens of imperialism have come home to roost, yet Brigitte's vision of *la douce Normandie* excludes a knowledge of France's colonial history, of its injustices, its oppression. Why should immigrant workers be so angry, so demanding? They shouldn't expect us to take on their culture. They should take on ours.

I can't love this part of her. I reject it. The godchild in me embraces the godmother in her. Our other selves don't touch.

My beloved aunt. Now you have cancer. Perhaps you will live for another five years. Just before Christmas, all your hair falls out. My beautiful aunt. You buy a wig. My mother tells me this over the telephone, for I haven't seen you for six months. I sit in the bathroom, crying. I'm angry with the doctors for invading your body with their harsh chemotherapy and radiotherapy, for making you nauseous and weak, for making all your hair fall out, for preparing to cut your breast off. You, who so respect science, accept this treatment. You say on the telephone: I'm determined not to die yet.

I come to see you. A brief weekend visit in late January, when snow-filled skies press down on the house and icy winds shake it. You say to me: The walls are fainting. You don't like your wig: I should have bought a necklace instead, the price it cost me. You wear a blue wimple to sleep in, and by day a scarlet scarf knotted behind your head: This is more comfortable, but it keeps slipping. I have to be careful when I go out. Young people are frightened by a bald woman. You scratch your skimpy eyebrows, formerly thick and black: Look, they're falling out too. Soon I'll have none left.

You look younger than ever. Illness has gentled you, let

148

you accept being looked after, opened you to the realisation of how much people love you. The phone rings constantly: your friends calling you. Women friends and neighbours from the village come in and sit with you, bringing you news, pots of home-made blackberry jam. You lie back in your low chair, talking about the cancer, how you feel. You don't care any more about dust in the corners, the washing-up. You call to me from your bedroom, where you lie, exhausted and faint.

– Leave cooking the lunch. Come and talk to me.

Your face is soft, smiling.

– On the day they told me I had cancer, you say, stroking the cat: I bought a new hat and then I went out dancing.

You can't make it to evening Mass, so I go for you. The church is freezing, almost empty. My pew has a hook for men's hats, women's gloves. The priest and tiny congregation caterwaul through the limp melodies of the modernised Liturgy, utter a watery poetry full of vague clichés, banalities. The rollcall of glorious virgins – Felicity, Perpetua, Agatha, Lucy, Agnes, Cecily and Anastasia – is no longer sung. I'm glad to be home again with you, helping you search your recipe book for *tarte Tatin*.

Tomorrow, Monday, when I'll have gone back to England, the surgeon will give you the date of the operation. Tonight, you're giving a feast. You come into the kitchen to show me how to clean and open the oysters. You instruct me on how to prepare the crab. You teach me the necessity of keeping on creating. You teach me how to accept your death.

C—R

Cancer. The unspeakable word. The word refused by the family. The word whispered in corners but never mentioned on the telephone. Now it's the word that Brigitte utters frequently. A new definition of herself.

CADICHON

Cadichon. The name of the Spriets' donkey. Ancient, amiable, docile, he allows us to mount him and ride him around the farm. He has to be whacked to make him move. Sometimes six of us small brutes sit astride him at once. Sometimes Monsieur Spriet harnesses him to the old two-wheeled trap kept in the coach-house. We arrange ourselves gingerly along the two seats with their worn coverings of leopardskin, distributing our weight evenly so that we won't tip over. Then we're off, wheeling rapidly between the cornfields, rushing through corridors of rustling gold, racing into the unknown, the depths of the farm.

CALVADOS

Calvados. Brandy made from cider apples. Sipped, in tiny glasses, after Sunday lunch. Made on the Spriets' farm, and named after Falstaff, who is supposed to have once stayed there.

CAMEMBERT

Camembert. The round cheese with a rough chalky coat which Brigitte scrapes off before serving it. We eat it for breakfast, often also at lunch and supper.

– When you buy a Camembert, Brigitte instructs us: you must smell it and press it to see if it is really ripe. The inside gushes out, yellow and runny, over the plate. You just eat it. You don't fiddle about with it. None of this Robert Carrier nonsense about deep-frying it in breadcrumbs.

CAUDEBEC

Caudebec. The small town in which my mother is born. The site of the *bac* (ferry) for crossing the Seine en route to Rouen and a picnic lunch in the forest. Also the site of a fine Gothic cathedral, its portals set with tiers of stone saints. We are proud of Caudebec, because it is our mother's birthplace, and beautiful enough to be worthy of her. Mum confers interest and dignity on the town, on the cathedral, on the Seine itself (*Sein*, breast). Every year she gives us the great treat of boarding the ferry, going across the wide river to the other side.

CAULLE

Caulle. My mother's family name. My mother is now called Roberts: the name of my father's family.

CAUX

Le pays de Caux. The Caux region. The part of Normandy in which the family lives, inland from the coast stretching between Etretat and Le Havre. Flat landscape of wide high skies; farms surrounded by high screens of beech trees; long straight roads flanked by tall elms; cows grazing in the pastures; fields of oats, barley and wheat. The Seine loops between Le Havre and Rouen, edged by orchards of fruit trees, stone houses with pointed slate roofs, small châteaux, old half-timbered cottages with irises growing along the ridge of the thatch, the abbeys of Jumièges and St Wandrille. The fine August drizzle comes down, and our bare feet slither on the soles of our leather sandals. The banks on either side of the gravelled roads are thick with purple and yellow flowers, raindrops hanging in the long grasses and spilling against our knees. We clamber up to pick nosegays, eye to eye with the cows munching steadily behind the barbed wire fence.

CINÉMA

Cinema. Home movies. Grandpère has brought back from Canada a cine-camera, which is used by him and Brigitte to record and invent the doings of the family. Every summer, the night arrives when we ask to see some films after supper. The silver screen is pulled up and hung in front of the window, and the rounded massive projector placed on Grandpère's desk. Darkness. Brigitte clatters film cans. A whine, a purr. White beam of light slicing past our heads.

I learn about our history by seeing it on film. My memories are given to me by the screen. We have two main favourites: the film of Bernard and Anne-Marie's wedding; and the film of our early childhood. Brigitte, film editor, constructs wonderful narratives: a wedding; darkness; a bouquet of flowers; darkness; a newborn baby; darkness; candles on an invisible birthday cake being blown out one by one; more flowers. There are Margi and me, pushing dolls in prams round and round and then stopping to kiss each other passionately. There's Andy, fat and smiling, crawling across the parquet floor with a hearthbrush. There's Jackie in a fur Eskimo suit. There's Mum, glamorous in a short fur coat, her dark hair pinned up in swoops and rolls, and Dad, in shirt-sleeves and Fair Isle pullover, leaning grinning on his spade outside our half-built house. There's Brigitte, in Hawaii, wearing a grass skirt and swaying her hips.

Brigitte, camerawoman and director, doesn't show murder directly on screen. Yet I know I've attempted it. There's my three-year-old brother Andy at Bernard's wedding, strutting with a thick bandage on his hand and arm. Every year, as we watch this film, the grown-ups coo: Poor Andy, however did it happen? I tremble in the darkness, waiting for Andy to denounce me. Every year, all through my childhood and adolescence. I know I tried to kill Andy. I pushed him over in the cellar, wanting him to die, and he slashed his hand on broken glass. Why doesn't he speak? What's he waiting for? Finally, aged twenty-seven, I ask him: Didn't I try to kill you when you were three? Surprised, he replies: You weren't anywhere near me, I fell over all by myself.

After the age of ten, after the onset of menstruation, breasts, frizzy hair and spots, I appear less on film, I flee the camera. Sometimes it catches me, scuttling rapidly across the lawn, squinting into the sun at the back of a family group. Who is this hideously embarrassed girl with plump knees under her unflattering brown shift dress with a gilt belt, frowning, ugly? I remember how much she hated herself, her rounded body and shiny childish face. I remember how desperately she yearned to be pretty and confident. She leaves fleeting traces: an elbow, a snub nose. She hides. Smiling bravely. Pleading: please don't look at me. I look at myself aged five, aged fifteen, aged twenty, and feel so protective of that clumsy surface I put up to shield myself from the gaze of others. All through my childhood and adolescence I draw obsessively: pictures of lovely naked women. I still do; but now they are allowed to have big swinging breasts, curving thighs, genitals, furry triangles of hair.

CRÈME

Cream. A staple in our diet. The cream here is very thick, slightly yellowish, slightly salty. Fresh. You can't find cream like this anywhere in England. We eat it poured over beans, over cod, over artichokes, over potatoes. It is unbelievably delicious.

The milk, which we fetch from the farm down the road every morning, has to be boiled before it is fit for drinking. Grandmère skims off the cream, which rises to the surface as a thick skin, and keeps it in a glass bowl in the fridge. After a week or so, there is enough cream for her to make her special cake *gâteau à la peau de lait*, a sort of rough rich sponge with a golden crust. We eat it for supper, with home-made pear conserve.

CRIQUETOT L'ESNEVAL

Criquetot L'Esneval. The name of the village where the family lives. Not just a geographical place: a place in the heart, in the psyche. My mother's home. The past. A way of life. A system of values. A group of people we refer to with respect and love.

The village straddles main roads that lead to Fécamp, to Goderville, to Le Havre, to Etretat. Around its outskirts lie the farms, straggles of old cottages. Its centre is simple, and small. The main street contains a few shops, the post office, the blacksmith's where the horses are shod, a bar we never go into, and the imposing neoclassical front of the *mairie* with its double stone staircase which we dare each other to run up and down. The *place* behind has the back of the *mairie* on one side, shops on the others. The haberdasher's, run by an ancient mademoiselle in velvet neckbands. The ironmonger's, full of radiant silver

154

buckets, tools, pottery. Madame Le Fevre's dim, cool grocery smelling of ripe melons to which we come with our stoppered glass jar to have it filled with fresh cream from the great vat in her cupboard. On Tuesdays the fish-woman sets her baskets outside, and we have mussels for lunch.

The church is just beyond the *place*, with a smelly men's lavatory, screened by corrugated iron, attached to its backside. A huge church, dark, with cold stone floors, smelling of incense, set with statues of saints and stained-glass windows whose images I know off by heart. After High Mass has ended, everyone collects outside in groups, talking, exchanging news. Certain families we shake hands with. Others we don't. Everybody knows who everybody else is: the 'good' families, the farmers of 'good' family, the farmworkers and farmers lower down the social scale. A red face and hands, a raw best blue suit, mark a man off from a lady in pleated silk. Then we go to the *pâtisserie* to buy galette for a late breakfast, cakes for lunch. Grandpère likes *babas au rhum*. When I choose *réligieuse*, a double round éclair with brown icing decorated with little tongues of cream, Grandpère says solemnly: You see the nun? Those flames on her mean she is burning in hell. He stands up all through Mass; he doesn't kneel. I understand this: the boss of the household doesn't need to kneel in church. Tall and severe in his grey suit, he's more formidable than M. Le Doyen, the parish priest. When I faint at Holy Communion, weakened by the obligatory fasting from midnight, by the long hours of kneeling and standing in the stuffy church, Grandpère picks me up and carries me out. I'm so ashamed of myself, so humiliated (my sister tells me: your knickers were showing), and Grandpère teases me to cheer me up: *Tu es tombée dans les pommes*, he explains: you have fallen in the apples.

The village is not beautiful, does not feature in tourist

brochures. This is of supreme unimportance, because it's the place where Grandpère and Grandmère and Brigitte live, the place we live in during the long summer holidays. We don't look for beauty in such a place. It is familiar, familial, ordinary, interesting. It is France, *tout court*. Not abroad. Home. The village is the people who live and work in it, whom we know, whose houses we visit.

Our house is a little way out of the village, on the Fécamp road, standing on a high grassy bank that Brigitte has tamed and sown with flowers. Blue and pink hydrangeas rear in front, redcurrant bushes along the wall at the side. The shutters are dark green. Geraniums are everywhere: spilling out of the windowboxes and out of the old wooden sabots hung on either side of the front door. The kitchen leans at one side. Three small windows in the roof.

The village changes, ancient cottages come down, replaced by concrete villas. An old people's home is built. The roads are widened, the verges lopped. Some of the ancient walled kitchen-gardens, with their rows of lettuces and sweet peas and gladioli and cabbages, are replaced by little plantations of hideous ornamental cypresses, stifling open displays of gravel, regimented beds of scarlet begonias, fences of looped chains. The village looks more like a suburb now. Tidier. Cleaner. Of course this means a higher standard of living, but, sentimentally, I miss the old ramshackle charm, the miraculous shrine on one of the back roads heaped with babies' shoes, the women sitting outside their little houses at sunset shelling peas together, the village pump from which we fetched water when our well ran dry, the ancient half-timbered tenement leaning against the church in which a dirty old woman lived. This proves how much of a tourist I've become, how I seek for the picturesque, how I don't live there any more.

Nous n'irons plus au bois,
Les lauriers sont coupés –

When Grandpère and Brigitte die, when the house is sold, as I suppose it will have to be, Criquetot will be a different place. We shall be totally absent from it, and its life will flow on without us. I know few of the village families now. I used to say hello to everyone I met. Now I'm a stranger there, met not with welcome but with indifference. My mother, who visits her father and sister several times a year, as often as she can afford on her earnings as a part-time teacher of evening classes (she's over sixty, can't teach in schools any more), still knows quite a few of the village people. She urges them, when she meets them in the butcher's or the baker's, to come and visit Grandpère, who is so lonely. But few of them do.

FRANÇAIS

French. The French language. My mother's tongue. My mother-tongue, that I take in along with her milk. The language of my childhood in France (the language of my childhood in England is another matter). My tongue lapping at pleasure. Hearing French spoken suddenly, in the street in London, or on top of a bus, makes me tingle with that pleasure all over again. The French I speak today is a ragbag of influences: the correct politenesses of the rituals of daily family life; the phrasing and archaisms of the novels by Gide and Mauriac I read as an adolescent; the utterances of relatives; the slang words taught me by my young cousins.

Bits of French buzz out of books of poems, and stick on me. *Douce mélancolie et harmonie du soir. Mais priez Dieu que tous nous veuille absoudre. Homme libre, toujours tu chériras*

157

la mer. De la musique avant toute chose. Poète, prends ton luth. Rappelle-toi, Barbara.

We pray in French at Mass. *Je vous salue, Marie, pleine de grace.* Religion feels different in French, a light elegant flavour like a soufflé in our mouths:

> *Le matin dans la clarté*
> *Le Christ est ressucité.*

We sing French songs as we tramp along the roads on our walks. *Au clair de la lune, mon ami Pierrot, prête-moi ta plume pour écrire un mot.* We sing rounds, too, the four children, my aunt keeping time. *Mordis sois-tu, carilloneur, que Dieu créa pour mon malheur.*

Ma petite poison, croons a neighbour to her baby: *ma petite poison.*

GLOSSAIRE

Glossary. According to the *Shorter Oxford English Dictionary*: 'a list with explanations of abstruse, antiquated, dialectal, or technical terms; a partial dictionary'.

To gloss: to explain away; to read a different sense into; to veil in specious language; to render bright and glossy.

GRANDMÈRE

Grandmother. Grandmère's name is Michelene. Mum and Brigitte and Grandpère call her Maman. Dad calls her Mère.

I do not know her well. Her thoughts and feelings remain

158

remote to me when I'm a child. She's busy running the house, living her social life as one of the ladies of the village. Her power is gently expressed, but you feel it: the house is her domain. She's not cuddly and affectionate like my English grandmother. I can see that her husband and daughters love her tenderly, but I don't get close enough to her to do so. She belongs to Brigitte, anyway. Brigitte is the one who goes into her room to talk to her, when she's having breakfast, or resting. We see her mainly at meals, which are a formal and collective affair. She's gently humorous in the face of Brigitte's possessiveness. She's sweet. She dresses in soft colours, soft fabrics. She's fragile.

She's often not well. Perhaps that sets her a little apart from the noisy children. One summer, she goes into hospital for a nameless operation. We're not told what's wrong with her. We're taken to visit her, told we must be utterly quiet. We tiptoe along the empty hushed corridors of the clinic, hover in the doorway of her room. Brigitte sits on her bed, holding her hand, love and anger and tears mixed up in her face. We're talking to Mum. Brigitte hushes us crossly: can't we hear that Grandmère is trying to sing *Ma Normandie* for us? We have made too much noise trooping into the hospital; going out, we must be even more like mice. That summer is particularly full of trouble and tension, centred on Grandmère's illness. Brigitte is very upset, and takes it out on Mum and Dad. Nana, our English grandmother, has also come to stay, and to help look after us. Brigitte is jealous of her, and shows it. Nana takes us out blackberrying. The relief, to be out of the house. There are too many of us. We take up too much space.

When she's well, Grandmère enjoys her rituals. She puts on her hat, takes her purse and her parasol, and goes into the village to shop, stopping to chat to all the people she knows and to enquire after their families. Or she goes to visit two poor widows: Madame La Flandre and Madame Avisse. She does a lot of good works: visiting, giving money to charity. Sometimes other ladies from the village come to tea, wearing hats, ladies of a certain class. Not the butcher's wife, for example. They sit in the salon, sipping their tea, nibbling little home-made biscuits and cakes. They address each other formally: Madame Caulle; Madame Le Forestier; Madame Spriet. To me these visitors are frightful women, so mincing and polite, a female mafia discussing diseases and marriages. I'm a tomboy. I'll never be one of them. I don't know how to attain their heights of femininity. Don't want to. It frightens me.

My mother is not one of them, either, though she sits there with them. Here in this house, I can see Mum as a girl again, sitting talking to her mother, a beautiful sturdy girl with brown shoulders above her cotton sunfrock. Mum lives in a wider world, goes out to work for her living, has travelled, dyes her blowing hair golden blonde, has been to university. Sitting here among these village matrons in their expensive ugly dresses and jackets, she simply doesn't fit. I'm suddenly glad we're half English, though I spend half my time in England defending the fact we're half French.

When we come down in the mornings, we kiss Grandmère, once she's up, and she remarks, in what's meant to be a kindly fashion, on how we are looking today: *Mimi a bonne mine aujourd'hui*, she will say, or: *Mimi n'est pas bien coiffée*. I wriggle; labelled, pinned down. One day she remarks how white and ill Margi looks, and my mother whispers: *Ce sont de mauvais jours pour elle*. This means having a period. Margi also hates having her appearance commented on. We're both of us awkward in our teenage, and we don't know what we can do about it.

Grandmère suffers increasingly from heart disease, though this is never discussed in front of us. At mealtimes she takes different coloured pills, swallowed down with a glass of water, and the contents of glass ampoules sawn in half by Brigitte with a razor blade. She eats special, different food. She mustn't eat salt. This plump, capable, white-haired person suddenly becomes a chronic invalid, her head poking forward and down, her belly swelling, her whole body thickening. She speaks little.

I leave home in 1967, to go to university. Over the next ten years I visit Criquetot irregularly, infrequently. I don't get to know Grandmère. I still don't know who she is. I don't remember her dying, her death. Grandpère tells us he doesn't want us to come to the funeral, so we stay away.

I think that my grandmother is the house. The storehouse of food and plenty. The cupboards stocked with sheets and tablecloths, tea and dinner services, boxes of silver cutlery and black-handled knives brought out for best occasions. She is still there.

Brigitte says to me in her jealous mourning: I think your mother grieved more for Nana's death than for Grandmère's. I think she was closer to Nana. My mother loved them both. She has a big heart. Plenty of room for both her mothers.

GRANDPÈRE

Grandfather. The maker. The creator, whose capable hands invent surprises for children: a tree-house, a slide, a cart, a giant papier-mâché whale, a wigwam. God is a grandfather, a carpenter, who delights in making, from his storehouse of bits and pieces, whatever's needed by the women in the household, by the children.

Grandpère is very tall, and spare, with fierce blue eyes under tufted brows, thick silky white hair, long arms, beautiful hands with long fingers. He is usually busy: carving, sawing, planing, nailing, glueing.

After lunch he sits in his red armchair by the table at the window and packs his pipe with tobacco, pressing it down in the bowl, applying a lighted match from the big Gitanes box, drawing, sucking. We bring him Three Nuns from England. He keeps his tobacco in a wooden box with a roll top, like a desk, and his instruments for cleaning his pipe, one silvery and spike-tipped, one like a thin spoon, laid out on a big square ashtray. The table is covered with his copies of the *Journal de Criquetot*, and the copy of *Le Figaro* that the pharmacist leaves for him every morning on the windowsill. (The pharmacist's wife, by the way, is so thrifty that she sews little patches on to the borders of the sheets to save them being worn away by her husband's bristly chin overnight.)

Upstairs is Grandpère's study, hung with old maps and charts of the port of Le Havre where he has spent most of his working life as an engineer. Here he writes his articles on local history, archaeology, topography, folklore. Also his short autobiography, which he entitles *Souvenirs d'enfance*. At one time we try to get it published. Without success. So it circulates just among the members of the family.

Grandpère eats his breakfast in the kitchen; usually before the rest of us are up. Big cup of *café au lait* into which he dunks his bread; crumbs swept neatly off the oilcloth patterned with wreaths of flowers. The tiles on the floor are scrolled with blue and yellow. The cat, Chouchou the Fourth, sits here, waiting for a snack.

After my breakfast I go to the lavatory upstairs. The windows, with their attached muslin-frilled curtains, have been flung wide to the view of sky and trees and fields, and the whole room smells deliciously of Grandpère: eau-de-Cologne and pipe tobacco and shit. These smells, anywhere in the world, bring him back to me immediately. Now that he's had the heart attack and strokes, he can't climb the stairs any more. His little dressing-room, opening off his bedroom on the ground floor, has been turned into a bathroom for him. This is the place to which we come with our cut and bleeding knees to have iodine put on by Grandmère. We are proud of the red stain on our skin: a decoration to be flaunted, bizarre as a tattoo. Grandmère's bed is still here, under the window. Piled with cushions, it acts as sofa. How chilly, how chastely tidy, how spotless this room is, with its grey marble fireplace, its gold-framed oil paintings, its little buttoned and frilled armchair, its carved cupboard, its jardinière of ferns and aspidistra. Grandmère's no longer in it, but it's still her room.

Grandpère is a patriarch. The absolute head of the family. The law-maker. The judge. Lunch must be on the table at one o'clock sharp. The tall clock in the corner chimes out the time, and one of us beats the gong in the hall. During these summer holidays we eat in the glass veranda, floored with speckled yellow tiles, at the back of the house. Children must eat neatly, speak only when addressed, never fidget or giggle. We three girls, trading good behaviour for love and approval, help serve and clear away the meal, trained by my aunt how to take away the dirty plates from the left and offer the clean one from the right. We while away the interminable interval before we can run out into the garden by moulding our bread into greyish pellets and figurines, daydreaming, whispering. My brother lacks these sensible tactics, draws attention to himself by talking too loudly, complaining of

163

boredom, answering back. Once he is shut in the coal cellar for three hours.

Nor does my father fare much better. The conversation at table is only in French, rapid and collective talk which Dad can't follow, though we can. The others have little patience with his slowness, and don't hide this. Nor do they approve of his eager gulping of soup (it's all right for Grandpère to make a noise drinking his), his liking for butter on bread, his quick swallowing of wine, his laying the table with the spoons facing the wrong way round. Dad does the washing-up after meals while we dry and put away. My aunt comes round afterwards to check he's done it properly, inspecting the porcelain sink for drip marks, the interiors of saucepans for traces of grease. Pouncing with a triumphant cry when she discovers a smear.

Dad's an Englishman. An outsider. Not one of the Caulle family. He tries so hard, making laborious French conversation with Grandpère about all the things he knows will interest him, being kind and polite to Grandmère, teasing and complimenting Brigitte on her looks, her clothes, her cooking. He can't realise how we ache in sympathy for him, that we feel his hurt; for we can't let him know that we have witnessed his humiliation, that we squirm for him, how much we pray that this lunchtime everything will go well, that there will be no trouble, no *sotto voce* remarks in French by my aunt on his awkwardness, on his manners, that he won't challenge Grandpère too openly on the latter's opinions of the trade unions, the youth of today, the English.

Grandpère praises me for the drawings I do. He scolds me harshly for daring to appear at the lunch table with mascara on my eyelashes, and I run out of the room crying. When my first novel comes out, he reads it. Part of it is set in

Normandy, and he's delighted to be able to point out the details I've got wrong.

— *Eh bien, ma fille*, he growls: the labourers did it *this* way, the hay-making. And he gives me a proper explanation. The heroine of the novel is a lesbian. In Grandpère's eyes I am now a woman of experience, and so, anti-clerical, he treats me to some of his scandalous stories about priests preaching in the pulpit with piss-pots hidden under their robes. He pours me wine, no longer mixing it with water: *tu es une fille sérieuse.*

Arthritis strikes. Grandpère can't move much. He hauls himself about on sticks.

Brigitte and I decide to take him for an outing in the car. I suggest visiting André Gide's grave, which is just up the road at Cuverville. All the way there, Grandpère, dressed in his navy beret, tweed jacket, blue jersey and blue and white striped shirt, grips his stick in one hand and waves the other in the air.

— *André Gide! Mais c'était un salaud! Un salaud!*

— *Pourquoi, Grandpère?*

— *Il était responsable, lui, ce salaud, pour des millions de jeunes suicidés, je te le dis* —

On the way back, we go to lay a fresh bouquet on Grandmère's grave in the village cemetery, the square walled place thick with crosses which we can see from the bathroom window. Brigitte and I fill a plastic watering can from the tap in the corner, top up the vases on the grave, arrange the flowers we have brought. Grandpère waits for us in the car.

When I leave, to go back to London, Grandpère presses a hundred and fifty francs into my hand.

He bursts into tears.

— *Ça peut être la dernière fois. Je ne sais pas si je te verrai encore.*

The steamroller stroke flattens and thins him, and the strong heart he rides on kicks and bucks, throwing him. Now he is the king of a small country: the red armchair. Beyond it, the household clicks and revolves, and he frets, not knowing what is going on.

His blue eyes are still fierce. His white hair is still silky and thick. Now it falls in long waves around his face, giving him the look of a beautiful old child.

He has learned to talk again. Sometimes his mouth stops and works, and the sound won't come, and he clenches his hands on the arms of his chair. I place my chair close to his, so that I can lip-read as well as listen.

Above his blue jersey his face is the same, and yet not the same. Is that because of age, and illness? Or because I am not frightened of him any more?

He looks back, with tears.

– *J'ai fait si peu de ma vie.*

He weeps, his brown mottled hand placed trembling over his eyes.

– *Tout est fini.*

He presses his handkerchief to his eyes. When he removes it there is still water shining in the brown creases of his skin.

– *Je n'ai pas le courage de vieillir.*

I take his hand in mine.

He gestures at the green glass beer bottle on the table beside his chair.

– *Une chose qui a été faite doit pas être jetée.*

Now we're both crying. Brigitte's sharp ears are on the alert: she bustles in from the kitchen, angry at me for letting Grandpère get upset.

– What's going on here? What's going on?

The only way she can cope with looking after Grandpère

singlehanded as well as working at her job in Le Havre is to be busy, practical, efficient. Grandpère needs to talk and to be listened to, and she hasn't got time. He has quarrelled with most of the people in the village over the last few years, and so he has practically no visitors.

– You can't imagine how terrible it is, she tells me: sitting here at night, when Grandpère's depressed and irritable. I'm so alone. I'm so lonely.

Lunchtime. Brigitte hauls Grandpère from his chair. His tall stooped body totters. His long legs look as though they will collapse. She supports him. He leans on her, and holds on to a small wooden chair. He creeps across the carpet to the dining table, lowers himself slowly and heavily into his chair, in Grandmère's old place.

– Don't watch him eat, Brigitte has warned me: he can't bear people knowing that he needs help with his food.

His spoon wobbles its way to his lips. Brigitte cuts up his bread for him. He spills his soup. He insists on his big white napkin being fastened to the front of his blue jersey by two large wooden clothes-pegs, waving away the two tiny plastic ones Brigitte offers him as an alternative. He spreads the other end on the tablecloth, and watches his soup-plate being set down on it again.

– *Tu vois*, he tells me: *je ne peux rien faire pour moi-même.*

Tears of anger spill down his face. He is distraught by his weeping, and cries more. I start to tease him and to crack jokes, and he cheers up a little.

At the end of the meal he instructs Brigitte to fetch a bottle of champagne. He watches her critically as she opens the door of the *bonnetière*, sets tall crystal *flutes* on a silver tray, brings them back to the table, uncorks the bottle, pours foaming champagne into each glass. The ritual must be performed, as it always has been, in exactly the right way, with dignity, with delicacy and grace.

He holds his glass in his trembling hand. He toasts me. He welcomes me to his house.

Brigitte joins me in the kitchen after she has settled him back in his chair, and we do the washing-up. I remember where everything goes: the enamelled yellow saucepans on to their rack over the humming fridge, the bread into the bottom drawer, the plates on to their shelves in the cupboard on the wall by the window. I put my arms around Brigitte and hug her, and she hugs me back. Except when we visit, she's got nobody to hug. The other teachers at school are all married, busy with their families, and don't visit her.

Going back into the sitting-room, I see that Grandpère's flies are undone, and that the covered basket I noticed earlier behind his chair is now on a stool in front of him, a wide-necked plastic bottle poking out from it. I tiptoe through the room so that Grandpère won't know I've seen him.

Grandpère's asleep. Two girls from the village, shrill and cheerful, have arrived to help Brigitte with some sewing. Later the priest will come, bringing Communion, and will stay just five minutes. These are the afternoons I remember so well: the absolute order of the house, the regular breathing, the women sewing and talking, the ticking of the grandfather clock.

On my latest visit, he's tired, subdued. The presence of a full-time nurse, now that Brigitte is no longer strong enough to look after him, seems to have helped him accept his ageing. He doesn't cry. He doesn't rage. He whispers: *Tout est fini.* He points out the baked salt and flour sculptures that he and the nurse have made together. He teases the nurse at supper for taking only two helpings of pudding. He smiles at me with great sweetness, his blue eyes shining, when I go

into his bedroom to wish him goodbye. His skin is very soft.
I kiss him gently on both cheeks. He's had his early morning
tea. Now, helpless, dignified, propped on white pillows, he's
waiting for breakfast. It's still dark outside the closed shutters.
He whispers: *Merci d'être venue. C'était un grand plaisir.* All night
long, the cat's been dancing about the room, worrying a mouse.
Grandpère laughs.

GRENIER

Granary. The storehouse. The place where things are made.
The place where Grandpère works. Where treasures are
piled up: home-made shallow boxes of paper, string, nails,
pine-cones; jars of brushes, tins of paint; racks of carpentry
tools; trays of electrical spare parts; reels of straw and raf-
fia for re-caning the seats of chairs; bottles of varnish and
turpentine. The boxes sit on shelves, stacked one above the
other, unnamed, closed, mysterious; masked with dust. From
the outside, the *grenier* looks quite small. Inside, it is enormous,
its far end impenetrable, swallowed in darkness; endless. In
my dreams I fumble my way to the end of the *grenier*, to where
the oldest memories of the family, the earliest relics, are stored,
to where the floor dissolves and I am falling, falling, into a new
country that is neither France nor England. Always I wake up
too soon. Before I land.

Grandpère's kingdom is high up in the sky, reached by a
ladder-like staircase, open slats of wood, a shaky rail. Its outer
wall, plastered a creamy yellow, is faced with criss-crosses of
timber. Through the open door, as I sit on the top step, I can
see Grandpère seated at his wooden work table, mending a
broken china cup, amber glue oozing between his fingers on
to the blue and white glaze. Looking the other way, I see

white clouds and blue sky, wind in the cracks. Below me, the high garden hedge, cows noisily swallowing grass with a slapping of jaws. White cows for milk, Grandpère explains: brown for tea, and black for coffee. The church bells, swinging in the steeple half a kilometre away across the fields, give the quarter-hour in long rolling chimes. Summer can mean lying face down on my bed sobbing with rage; it can also mean this high windy solitude, the bells dividing the blessedly long and lonely morning, a book in my lap.

Behind the *grenier*, at right angles, is the high bank, set with a close row of towering beeches, that shelters the farm next door. The trunks of the trees are grey-brown, glossy. They turn away the active August wind, shine in the drizzle.

Underneath the *grenier* staircase, between the field hedge and the hedge bounding my grandparents' garden, is a long narrow gap filled up with weeds and rubble: a wilderness where only we children go; one of our secret places. We crouch here, draw the greenery over our heads, confident of being unseen by the adults, and become archaeologists, turning up shards of pottery, bones, bits of painted tile. Or we scoop at the damp earth with our hands and make clay pots and dishes which we decorate with violets stuck about the clumsy rims. A favourite aunt, invited to enter our hiding-place and inspect our art-works gives them a cursory glance and suggests smashing them as it is teatime.

Below the *grenier* is the coal cellar, and, next door, the wine cellar, cool dim apartment with an earth floor, no windows, and a wooden door locked with a great iron key. Sent from the kitchen to fetch two bottles of cider for Sunday lunch, I come down the narrow path skirting the lawn, stepping past the curly fronds of fern that reach from the flowerbeds, loaded with dew, to pick at my red cotton dress, parting the bushes that lean together at the entrance to the tiny courtyard. To my left the *grenier* steps; ahead of me the two cellar doors: to my right the door of the shed in which Grandpère stores lumber, his old bicycle, the slide and the papier-mâché whale he has made for us; and the door of the disused lavatory. We are not supposed to go in here but we do: another hiding-place. We lift up the wooden lid from the plank-like seat, and peer into the black hole smelling of ancient shit. Now I enter the dark wine cellar, propping open the door to let in a shaft of light; scent of earth, mustiness, dust. I pick out two unlabelled green glass bottles from the iron rack on the side wall, bear them back to the house where I wipe off their film of cobwebs with a cloth and set them, uncorked, in the big fireplace in the *salon*.

The *salon* bears witness to Grandpère's ingenuity, to his use of carpentry tools kept in the *grenier*. It used to be two separate rooms. During the Occupation, the *sales Boches* inform the family that since they have two downstairs rooms, they will have to have a German officer billeted on them. Overnight, with the help of friends, Grandpère knocks the two rooms into one, building a wooden arch between them. When the Germans arrive in the morning, they see that they have made a mistake. The officer lodges in one of the upstairs rooms. That's not quite so bad.

A mossy old statue, with the blurred features of a dancing goddess or nymph, used to lean against the cellar wall underneath the *grenier*. It vanished long ago. I don't know what happened to it.

LINGERIE

Linen-room. The first floor of the house, originally attics, is converted by Grandpère into bedrooms, bathroom, study, when he moves the family there from the little house in the middle of the docks at Le Havre. The staircase, narrow and steep, twists up abruptly from the little hall into a tiny landing. Back across the top of the stairs, over a little bridge, is my aunt's room, with the one my parents occupy next to it. Opposite are Grandpère's study, in which my brother Andy sleeps during the summer holidays, and the bathroom. The corridor bends away from here, just wide enough to let a body through, and turns a corner. At the end of this passage is what used to be the maid's tiny room, where my elder sister Jackie sleeps, and then finally the *lingerie*.

In summer, two little beds are set up here for my twin sister Margi and me. The rest of the year, this is the place where the ironing is done. The ironing table is covered with a thick grey blanket, a white sheet laid on top. The bulky iron sits in a steel cradle. Scorch marks, like rings of damp, on the white cloth. The smell of cotton and linen, dried outside in the sun and air, and the hot smell of ironing. White shirts sway on hangers. Sheets drop from a line suspended from the ceiling, white wings.

The magic room under the roof, that changes into our bedroom. Twin cotton bedspreads in faded paisley, pleasing worn red and yellow, a faint design. The roof slopes sharply down under the eaves, a window set in it, screened against mosquitoes. Between Margi's bed and the wall run cupboards built by Grandpère that house boxes of sewing material and old magazines. The wall alongside my bed, panelled in plywood, bears shelves of books: Mum's old schoolbooks, old exercise books. Grey or red cloth covers; strange typefaces cramped on the yellowing glossy pages. We find her adolescence here, her pencilled notes, her underlined words. Texts we cannot understand: Latin, Greek, chemistry, maths. My mother aged sixteen, seventeen. Long before we came into existence she had a life of her own. We finger the books.

The light-switch for the landing and corridor is just outside our room. The inevitable terror of coming upstairs in the dark draws nearer all day long. Up the black well of the stairs, feet finding the way across the landing, then down the blind inkiness of the passage to our bedroom. Something lurks there, waiting for me.

Press down on the china switch. Next terror to be negotiated: the large furry moths, with fat barrel bodies and clattering whirring wings, that beat from wall to wall and bang against the light-bulb. In those days I have no pity for trapped moths: I shout for my father to kill them. One night, just as we're falling asleep, there is a sudden whining, buzzing, metallic thumping. A moth we thought dead has resurrected itself and is screaming with pain in moth-language. Going to the lavatory in the middle of the night: I put it off as long as possible. The stairs are dark and invisible, and a white headless ghost runs up and down them, waiting for me. Back in bed, I stare at the huge wardrobe. Moonlight glimmers in the mirror on its door in strange shapes. The elaborate carved knot decorating its top changes into a hideous face that grimaces at me, teeth bared.

The mornings deliver me, with light and sun. In the afternoons I come up here, in the interval between the end of lunch and the time for going to the beach, when the women are sewing in the veranda and Grandpère and Dad are dozing, and I read and read. Reading means privacy, solitude, a room of my own, a world away from the family. I reconnect with my mother, aged sixteen, studying her chemistry textbook. Free time, time of my own. The need for this takes root here, in the *lingerie*.

173

MAISON DANS L'ARBRE

Tree-house. Grandpère builds us the tree-house, in the branches of the old apple tree at the foot of the garden in front of the *grenier*. A ladder leads up to our high fenced platform. We lounge here, all summer through. Our hideaway, which the grown-ups are not allowed to enter unless we invite them. Rows of dolls. Books. Dreams. Picnic lunches.

The apple tree grows diseased, and eventually has to be cut down. From its wood, Grandpère makes each of us four children a three-legged milking stool as a souvenir.

MOISSON

Harvest. *La fête de la moisson*, the harvest festival, is held in late August. For many years I don't realise that it's not an official Catholic feast like Christmas and Easter. It follows so logically upon them. It is their culmination.

The church is decorated with great swags and bouquets of braided golden corn, cornucopias of fruit and vegetables. The farmers are praised, their produce blessed. We all give thanks.

One year our celebration supper is held in the glass conservatory at the back of the Spriets' house, a great table, covered in white, stretching from end to end, and the talking and feasting going on underneath the great vine growing along the ceiling dangling bunches of purple grapes. Afterwards, there are fireworks in the courtyard outside, and dancing. Coloured Japanese lanterns sway in the trees, piercing the thick darkness. The young men treat us girls as adults, taking us in their arms and waltzing us away, giddy, drunk on pleasure.

NOCES

Wedding. Bernard, Mum's brother, is marrying Anne-Marie Spriet. One of the great events of these years. Better than the coronation of Queen Elizabeth, because it's local and we can join in.

Ten bridesmaids follow the bride in pairs, graded from tiny to quite big. Our hand-sewn dresses stick out like lampshades, white frilled tiers, and have small neat collars and puffed sleeves. We wear white net gloves and clutch our partners' hands. We've been told we mustn't let go. We carry little hooped baskets of white straw, which we use for taking the collection during Mass. One girl spills hers right across the floor. Also we wear narrow silver bracelets, the gift of the bridegroom. Anne-Marie's dress is white too, long and plain with a little collar and buttons down the front. Her long veil, streaming away from her small round flat headdress perched on her chestnut hair like a nurse's cap, is spread out between the ten bridesmaids and carried by us. Margi and I are five. We concentrate. Jackie is seven, more capable. Anne-Marie leans on her father's arm; he is wearing tails, a black bow-tie, a stiff shirt, a pointed collar. Madame Spriet, although it is only morning, is in full evening dress and furs. Bernard wears a double-breasted suit, and has gone into the church ahead of us. We stumble after Anne-Marie, gripping her long gauze tail. The black mouth of the church swallows her up, and then us.

My brother Andy, aged three, is an onlooker, like Dad. But he too, like the bride, is an object of interest, for his arm is bound up in a great bandage after he has fallen over and cut his hand open. The doctor has mended it with a metal clip.

All the guests stand talking and laughing on the great lawn, with low spreading cedars at its far end, in front of the Spriets' house. This lawn is where we play croquet, fielding the wooden balls from the long flowerbeds filled with white flowers and silver leaves. Now it's thronged with strangers. Lunch has been laid in the old coach-house. The major-domo, in full evening dress, stands in the doorway, calling out names, in pairs, and the men come forwards with crooked arms, to take the ladies in.

Gaiety. Dancing. The adults transformed from parents and relatives into relaxed playful young men and women. Mum looks beautiful in a swirly white nylon dress covered in large black spots, black high-heels. Brigitte wears red, sleeveless and figure-hugging. Dad's a boy, throwing Andy up and down in his arms, smiling. Grandmère is elegant and gracious, a fine lady. Grandpère is very tall, very handsome, in his dress-suit, his figure tall and erect, his white head towering. We bridesmaids, released from standing still and being good, tuck up our stiff skirts and race about, shrieking. Bernard and Anne-Marie, our former playmates and companions, have walked a little away from us, into a different place. They're more like the grown-ups now. We are celebrating this change. Very soon after, it seems to me, they are showing us their first baby, smothered in lace and wool wrappings in the height of summer, squalling and cross. To me it's as though they've been given a doll as a present. As a reward.

NOCES DE DIAMANT

Diamond wedding. My grandparents have been married for sixty years. There is a special Mass in the village church, attended by all the family (children, grandchildren, great-grandchildren, plus many other relatives) and friends, and many of the village families. My grandparents have special red velvet armchairs and prie-dieux set for them in the aisle. M. Le Doyen praises them, their example, in his sermon. He speaks of their lives here in Criquetot, and the lives of their children. He praises Brigitte for giving up so much in order to care for them.

Back at the house, the immediate family attends the *vin d'honneur*. Grandmère is very frail now, and can't cope with too many people. We toast her and Grandpère in champagne. Kisses and laughter and tears.

Lunch is at Charles and Monique Spriet's house. Charles's two unmarried sisters, Lou and Geneviève, live in the big house now. The Spriet parents are dead. Charles and Monique have restored an old half-timbered farmhouse in the grounds, and live there with their four children. There are thirty or so of us sitting around the table: family, old friends, the priest. At each place is a little gold sabot filled with gold flowers: symbol of my grandparents' house, which is called *La Sabotière*. We have printed menus. Two waitresses, in black frocks and tiny white aprons, serve us with salmon and roast lamb. Starched white tablecloth. Four different wineglasses at each place. Terrific noise of laughter and talking. This lunch is the real Mass: the celebration of this community of relatives, of the bond between us. I'm part of this huge, enduring, passionate family; yet my life in London also makes me an outsider. I'm so glad to be back amongst them all, yet I'll take flight as soon as this festival is over. I sit down at the end of the table, my back to the enormous rustic fireplace, and watch them all.

Lunch goes on for most of the afternoon. Bernard, as the son of the house, makes a long speech, and we all drink a toast in champagne. Mum, I'm pleased to see, also makes a speech.

177

Flown on wine and calvados, I stand on my chair and recite a poem by Baudelaire:

Mon enfant, ma soeur, songe à la douceur
d'aller là-bas vivre ensemble . . .
Là, tout n'est qu'ordre et beauté
luxe, calme, et volupté.

Grandmère, stricken by her last illness, has made an enormous effort to gather the strength necessary to be present at this day. She sings to us, in a tiny quavering voice. It is her farewell to us. This diamond wedding feast is our farewell to her. She dies soon afterwards.

PAIN BÉNIE DES HOMMES

The men's blessed bread: a sort of brioche, yeast dough made with butter and eggs. The feast of the *pain bénie des hommes* falls in the summer, between the Assumption and *la fête de la moisson*. The men of the village go up to the altar rails during Mass and receive this special bread, which they bring away in their hands. I wonder why the women don't receive it too. We're allowed to eat Grandpère's share, when he brings it home. Yellow, spongy, salty. A big piece we tear apart and share. It's all right for us to eat it, because it's not the body of Christ. It's a pagan communion, and we are the priests.

PLAGE

Beach. Almost every afternoon, after the washing-up has been done and the coffee drunk and the women have had their chatting and sewing while the men snooze, we go to the beach, leaving Grandpère and Grandmère behind. We pile into the car, Brigitte in the front passenger seat because she gets car-sick, Mum and the four kids squashed into the back. Usually we go to Etretat, eight kilometres away down the little valley of small rolling golden fields. The road gets narrower; the cliffs start to rise up, and we're there. Etretat is an old-fashioned Edwardian watering-place, with ancient tea shops and hotels, a covered market, tall red-brick houses faced with fancy designs in white stone, a long wide promenade overlooking the bay with its three dramatic arches of cliff, its old oyster beds, its pebbled beach and wooden beach-huts painted in worn pastel colours. The flag flying from the flagstaff is green, which means it's safe to bathe. We pick our way along the steep hill of round stones, and spread out our things.

We undress under towels, complicated wiggles. We children wear bubbly nylon suits laced at the back with long strings, and rope-soled canvas *espadrilles* to protect our feet. When we come out of the water, the knots in the laces of the *espadrilles* are difficult to untie. Back at home, we put them on the top of the well to dry, and they go hard as cardboard. The water is always icy. We race straight in; it's the only way. First the shriek at the cold shock; then frantic swimming in order to warm up. Usually the waves slap high and lively, and we dart up and down them. Or we hire a *périssoir*, a two-seater canoe, or paddle around in old inner tyres, black and enormous. Sometimes Mum and Brigitte don't swim, but stay on the beach knitting, and I don't understand their carefully coded explanations why. Tea on the beach tastes so good: gritty bright yellow lemonade, lengths of baguette with a piece of bitter dark chocolate stuffed down the middle. We lie back on Dad's old army blanket, heads propped on damp towels, feeling the sun's warmth enter our bodies. Or we look for pebbles with holes in, or ones shot through with glittering quartz, or pieces of green glass worn into emeralds. Treasures to bring back in our pockets.

Sometimes we climb up on to the cliffs and go for walks through the dry gorse in the keen salty wind, past the red summerhouses scalloped and fretted with white, the golf course in the distance. We stand on top of the highest cliff arch, named the *Chambre des Demoiselles*, whence a wicked baron once rolled his brides, one by one, in spiked barrels, down into the sea. Or we explore the far end of the beach where the fishing boats are drawn up and where the fishermen sit mending their nets amid piles of lobster pots. Some of the old boats have been turned into tiny cafés, with thatched roofs, where you can sit and eat sea food at night and listen to the waves pounding the beach just below while the juice of *moules* runs down your chin. Sometimes, at low tide, we scrabble around on the rocks covered in slippery green weed, poking for crabs, trying to prise off limpets, feet springing on sopping mess. Tunnels lead up from the base of the cliffs here, link up with the gun emplacements higher up. The floor of the cave is ribbed sand, white, damp and hard. We're forbidden to go far in. We might get lost, and never come out.

The beach means freedom from clothes, from most restrictions, from polite behaviour. Freedom to run, climb, swim, roll and yell. Freedom to dance in the water, to glide and float, to lie on the shingle at the water's edge looking up at the steep shelf of the beach while the waves break over me, half-submerged. Freedom to be languid, to dream.

I walk along the beach at low tide, inspecting the debris scattered along the tideline. A white lace glove. A pipe. A chipped blue enamel serving-dish. An apple core. A yellow novel. An old franc piece. A pleated white Terylene skirt.

A packet of rough brown lavatory paper. An amethyst and silver rosary.

I must put them into some sort of order. Make a list. The tide's turned, is coming in fast. My aunt's voice on the telephone: Yes, come and see us again soon. We'll have a good time. Just like in the old days.

Come back.

Vien.

About the author

Half-English and half-French. Michèle Roberts was born in
1949. Her permanent home is London. Author of two solo
collections of poetry, she has also co-authored four volumes
of short stories. Michèle Roberts has published six highly
acclaimed novels, of which her most recent, *Daughters of the
House* (1992), was shortlisted for the Booker Prize and winner
of the W.H. Smith Literary Award.